Jessie felt the hot water soothe her, physically and mentally, as she soaked luxuriously in the soapy tub. For the first time in weeks she relaxed, closing her eyes and breathing in the clean steam of the hot water.

Suddenly the bathroom door swung open. A man stepped inside.

Jessie reached for a nearby towel. "What the hell do you think you're doing?" she demanded. "Get out of here."

The stranger made no move to leave. He glanced over his shoulder at the open door. "If I was you, I'd bolt that door when I took a bath. Purely unsafe, ma'am."

In one quick movement Jessie reached for her converted .38 Colt, which lay on the towel bench. It was cocked and aimed at the man's belly before he could blink. "I think you'd better leave," she said through clenched teeth. . . .

WESLEY ELLIS

# LONE STAR

## AND THE BADLANDS WAR

A JOVE BOOK

LONE STAR AND THE BADLANDS WAR

A Jove Book / published by arrangement with
the author

PRINTING HISTORY
Jove edition / November 1983

ISBN: 0-515-07273-7

Jove books are published by The Berkley Publishing Group,
200 Madison Avenue, New York, N.Y. 10016. The words
"A JOVE BOOK" and the "J" with sunburst are trademarks
belonging to Jove Publications, Inc.

# LONE STAR

## AND THE
## BADLANDS WAR

# Chapter 1

The big house was perched improbably on a steep bluff overlooking the muddy town. It resembled one of those French chateaus that Jessie Starbuck had seen years ago in Europe, except that this one was not built on a lazy tree-lined river or amid a vast green estate—instead, it clung as tenaciously as a wild eagle to a sheer face of rock, towering over a dreary Dakota Badlands town called Augusta.

Jessie and her companion, Ki, approached Augusta on horseback, a torturous five-day journey behind them. The town's wide streets had been muddied by two days of autumn drizzle and presented an uninviting, sorry spectacle. Less than a year old, the Dakota Territory hamlet was a collection of clapboard and unpainted pine structures, three dozen or so, in various stages of construction or premature decay.

Above, the gravid gray sky promised more rain. Jessie pulled her slicker more tightly around her against the damp cold. She shivered slightly. "It can't be as bad as it looks," she said to her fellow rider. "Not that I expected it to be Austin or El Paso."

Ki, a lanky man with Oriental features, was also wrapped in a yellow rubber-coated slicker. "They must have a reason

1

to call this the Badlands," he replied with a gleam of humor in his dark eyes.

"No need to remind me. A hot bath and a hot meal and a good night's sleep are all I need. These animals are exhausted, too." She glanced up again at the big house on the bluff; against the heavy, gunmetal-gray sky it took on a sinister aspect. A finger of cold traveled down her spine. *I definitely need that sleep,* she thought.

A few bedraggled souls slogged through the streets from shop to saloon to home. Otherwise the town looked fairly deserted. They halted at a livery to see after the horses. The livery boy might as well have been a deaf mute for all the information they got out of him. They paid him a dollar in advance and instructed him to feed, water, and curry the animals. In return he gestured awkwardly toward the street when they asked where they could find a hotel.

Jessie gritted her teeth, tired and frustrated. The trip from the Circle Star ranch in Texas, her home, to the Dakota Territory had taken over two weeks, by rail to Rapid City and on horseback for the remaining hundred miles. It was rough riding through dangerous, unsettled hill and river country, but there was no other way; the Northern Pacific had not yet laid its steel rails along this route. Anyway, Jessie liked to spend time on the open trail, away from cities and towns, away from the cares of her ranch and her business responsibilities. For her, it was usually a time to renew her energies and to think things through. But this time it was different. She had come to no definite conclusion as to why she sensed that something was very wrong here and why she had ridden hard to get here so quickly, driving herself and Ki to the point of exhaustion....

"It must be this way," Ki said. He carried his saddlebag over his shoulder and slogged ahead of her across the viscid mud of the street. Jessie followed.

When occasion demanded it, she gladly let Ki lead. Riding with her half-Japanese, half-American companion and protector, she had a valuable asset she'd match against anything her enemies might throw at her. With Ki, she could feel secure enough to brave new territory as well as discuss her concerns with an intelligent, sympathetic man who understood her ways like no other man ever would. For Ki had been with her, and her father before her, for many years. A twinge of grief drove away the physical coldness.

She remembered the last time she had seen her father, Alex Starbuck, alive. Had it been so long ago? He had been a handsome, vital man even in middle age: tall, barrel-chested, with broad shoulders and a large, well-shaped head. His smile, his earthy yet authoritative speech—how she missed the man! And then he had been ambushed and brutally assassinated, his powerful body torn apart in a rain of bullets. His daughter lived on with only his memory—and a burning desire to avenge his death. A daunting task, but the great man, her father, deserved no less. He had taught her the meaning of family honor and loyalty, and she had learned her lesson well. Despite the occasional moments when Jessie felt like giving up, she never failed to rally to his memory and to renew her vow to ensure that he had not died in vain.

At a young age she had taken on a terrible responsibility, and she had to learn how to balance the twin tasks that went with being Alex Starbuck's daughter: to avenge his death and to preserve his legacy through the Starbuck fortune.

Luckily, Jessie had Ki at her side. Reaching back even further in time, she remembered when she was a little girl, and Alex Starbuck had first brought the young half-Japanese man to the magnificent Circle Star spread in West Texas. Then, as now, Ki was a tall man, slender, with gleaming, raven-black hair and smooth, pale skin. His eyes were his most intriguing and mysterious feature; they were black and almond-shaped and always drinking everything in. She hadn't

3

known then what to make of him, but over the years she had come to love him like a brother. There was no one in her life, since her father's death, who was as close to her as Ki. And until she found the man she would marry—a distant prospect—she expected to spend a lot more time with this quiet, intense man who had so many times proved his inestimable value in a fight. They had been through so many tough scrapes together. . . . But now was not the time for memories, she reminded herself. They had work to do here in the Badlands.

Jessie felt Ki's hand on her arm. "We're here," he said.

She looked up and brightened when she saw the sign above the door: AUGUSTA INN AND BATH HOUSE.

What passed for a hotel in Augusta had two rooms available. For six bits a night they had the dubious comfort of four walls, a straw mattress, and a porcelain pitcher and washbowl. Jessie skimmed off the dust floating on the water in the pitcher before pouring some out into the bowl and cleaning her hands and face. A lone candle flickered by the bed; the window was closed but the room was cold.

Ki was in his own room, next door. Jessie was grateful for these moments alone after their long trip. She looked into the blurred, yellowing mirror that hung crookedly on the wall over the pitcher. Her pretty, even features were gaunt with exhaustion, her red-gold hair lusterless and limp. God, she needed a bath! Nearly an hour later, having roused the lethargic clerk to heat some water, she stepped into an oversized zinc tub in a private cubicle in the downstairs bath house and began soaking away the grit and ache of the trail.

As always, she carried a bar of her own perfumed soap for just such occasions. The soap felt smooth and soft on her arms, breasts and legs, skimming the soft curve of her white flesh. The pleasure was almost sexual in its soothing intensity. For the first time in weeks she relaxed, closing her eyes and breathing the clean steam of the hot water. The saddle-weary miles melted from her and her mind roamed free.

At first there had been disquieting rumors that had found their way to Texas, where Jessie was overseeing preparations for the fall roundup at the vast Circle Star spread. Among the many Starbuck land holdings throughout the West, the family owned a five-hundred-acre stretch of cattle-grazing land along the Little Missouri River, here in the wild Dakota Territory. Her father had purchased it many years ago in hopes of eventually setting up a beef-breeding operation, and he had hired a man to tend a small herd there. Alex Starbuck had been cut down by the cartel before the plan was able to take final shape. But the seed herd and the land and the foreman were still here, and possibly—if those rumors had any merit—in danger.

The threat—if one truly existed—came from the man in that big house on the bluff, the Marquis de Beaumont, a transplanted Frenchman of tremendous wealth who was buying up land throughout the valley. The rumors concerned other ranchers who were not selling to the Marquis; they seemed to fall victim to misfortune more often than others, through cattle rustling and water poisonings and accidents that sometimes cost them their lives. Nothing had been proved, but the coincidences added up to dark suspicions that would not go away.

Jessie's source for her information was her man at the Slash S spread, the Starbuck property north of Augusta. Clark King was the man hired by her father a few years back to oversee the ranch and gradually increase the herd, until the time came when the Starbuck interests decided to place a full herd of a few thousand head on the Badlands range. From her father's correspondence and the surveyor's reports, Jessie knew that the land was rich grazing country with plenty of water, a perfect location for a large cattle-

5

ranching operation. Her father had had high hopes for the land before he died.

Jessie put that thought out of her mind and concentrated on the problem at hand. She had written to King herself to ask about the rumors, and the foreman had replied cautiously that other cattlemen were upset at recent events, but that he had not had any personal contact with the Marquis de Beaumont. He would report to Jessie any further incidents. He recommended that she come have a look for herself when it was convenient; King was anxious to expand the operation as soon as possible.

Discussing the matter with Ki, Jessie had decided to pay a visit to Augusta and the Slash S to see for herself what was going on. She didn't like the sound of it: the Marquis's money dealings, the cattlemen's uneasiness, King's wary tone in his letters. So, without announcing her plans in advance, she had left the Circle Star in West Texas and made her way up here with Ki to the Dakota Territory. Not that it was easy to keep such a secret for long—she knew that by the time they hit town, word would already have begun to spread.

She felt the hot water renewing her, physically and mentally, as she soaked luxuriously in the soapy tub. The responsibilities upon her slender shoulders were immense, and often she longed for a release from them. A private moment like this, in a hot bathtub, allowed her to think things through at her leisure, to put her troubles in their proper perspective. If only she had more time to deal with them all—as her father had. If only she were as strong and surefooted as he had been in his business dealings. She was learning—and quickly—but it would take time to gain experience, and sometimes she wondered if time was running out for her, as it had for Alex Starbuck.

Then, suddenly, the bathroom door swung open. A man stepped inside.

Jessie reached for a nearby towel, slipping it over her chest and turned to inspect the intruder. "What the hell do you think you're doing?" she demanded. "Get out of here."

He was a skinny man of average height, dressed in a black suit, with a low-crowned black felt hat tilted back on his head. His dark eyes took in the breathtaking sight before him, his hawklike nose inhaling the pleasant smells of a woman bathing. Jessie noticed that he carried a brace of Colt revolvers on a tooled cartridge belt around his narrow hips. He wore small-roweled spurs at the heels of pointed black boots.

"Beg pardon, ma'am," the man said, obviously feigning shock. "Didn't mean to barge in. I thought this room was empty—it's my regular room, this time of day." A gray ash dropped from the cigarillo dangling between his lips.

"Well, as you can see, the room is occupied," Jessie shot back. "I'm in it, and I wish you'd—"

"I can see that, ma'am." The stranger made no move to leave. He glanced over his shoulder at the open door. "If I was you, I'd bolt that door when I took a bath. Privacy is at a premium in these parts—this being about the only place in town a body can take a proper bath, and all sorts of unsavory characters roaming the streets—purely unsafe, ma'am."

Fuming, Jessie attempted to control her temper. But it was not easy. "I appreciate your concern, mister, but I'm telling you, you better get the hell out of here."

In one quick movement she reached for her converted .38 Colt, which lay on the towel bench. It was cocked and aimed at the man's belly before he could blink. "I mean it," she emphasized through clenched teeth.

The stranger did not flinch. In his long black coat, he looked like a well-dressed scarecrow. He said quietly, his eyes not moving from the barrel of her revolver, "You must be Miss Jessica Starbuck."

7

"What concern is it of yours?" Her eyes narrowed. She was getting mighty sick of this man, mighty fast.

"Well, I have something for you." Very carefully he pulled open his coat and with outstretched fingers lifted an envelope from an inside pocket. He dropped it on a chair near the door. Tipping his hat, he backed away, opening the door.

"Good day, Miss Starbuck," he said. "And happy bathing."

When the door closed behind him, Jessie emerged from the tub, dripping, and went to latch the door. She'd been stupid not to do it earlier, but she hadn't thought of it. What if the man had come to kill her? She would have been dead by now, despite having brought her revolver along. Stupid. She must remember to be extra careful here in Augusta, even while bathing—no, *especially* while bathing.

Back in the soothing water, she realized the man had not told her his name. And how had he known hers? Of course, as she had expected, word was out already about Ki and herself. And what was in the mysterious envelope? Jessie dried her hands and opened it. On an expensive piece of paper, embossed with a fancy European coat of arms, was an invitation to dinner—from the Marquis de Beaumont.

So, Beaumont had summoned her already; and she had been in town less than two hours.

Jessie finished her bath and went back upstairs to lie down on the lumpy bed, to try and catch some sleep. But sleep wouldn't come as the face of the intruder kept coming back to her. He had the look of a shootist, of a professional; and, despite his poor timing, he pretended to have the manners of a gentleman. It didn't make sense.

She collected and reviewed in her mind everything she knew about Augusta and the Little Missouri Valley. From what Clark King had related to her, Jessie knew that the Frenchman who called himself the Marquis de Beaumont had come into the Dakota Territory over a year ago, with big money and big ideas. He had founded the town, naming it after his wife, and built his gaudy mansion and started up a cattle operation that King and others estimated at more than four thousand head. That made him the biggest man around, and he wasn't averse to throwing his weight around when necessary.

Jessie had heard from King that the Marquis controlled the town of Augusta with an iron hand, financing its growth and development, opening the first bank, encouraging people to come and settle. And he had been surprisingly successful in a very short time. For, although the place didn't look like much now, she was aware that it was still new and still had limitless possibilities—if the people stayed on and made it work. But King emphasized that underneath it all there was a sense of unrest; the Frenchman had insisted from the beginning that his was a one-man show, that he called all the shots. That, of course, did not set too well with independent-minded Westerners, especially cattle ranchers, who were used to taking orders from no man.

Now, more than ever, she was anxious to meet with King, who could fill her in on the situation in more detail. And, unexpectedly, she would have her first audience with the Marquis this very evening.

She called the hotel clerk and sent him off with her dress to be cleaned and pressed. Always prepared for the unexpected when it came to her wardrobe, Jessie had packed a fancy dress for this trip, in case such an occasion presented itself. Meanwhile, she would try again to rest. Having laid her .38 Colt revolver on the stand beside the bed, she lay back and closed her eyes. A soft knock on the door brought her to her feet, the revolver in her hand. She went to the door and stood to one side.

"Who is it?" she called.

It was Ki. She let him in. "Sorry to disturb you, Jessie,"

he said, knowing she was bone tired.

"That's all right, Ki. I'm not having any luck getting to sleep."

"You must learn to clear your mind, Jessie. The body needs rest and must not be denied."

"Easy for you to say," she quipped with a smile.

"Not so easy. I, too, had to learn to allow myself the time to renew my energies in preparation for the task at hand. It is not an easy lesson to learn, but a necessary one."

"I'll try, Ki," Jessie assured him. Then she told him of her uninvited visitor in the bathroom. Ki's face clouded with concern, but she hastened to let him know that nothing had happened, other than the delivery of the invitation from Beaumont, which she shared with him.

Ki read it and said, "There's a lot the Marquis does *not* say—such as how he knew we were here."

"That's what I thought," Jessie agreed. "But I'll find out plenty tonight. And," she said, anticipating his objection, "I'll be careful."

Ki said, "I'll take a look around town while you're up on the bluff. Between us, we should be able to get a good picture of what's happening in these parts."

"And *you* be careful, Ki. I can't do anything without you."

As he headed for the door, he said, "Catch up on your sleep, Jessie. And dream of those good times we had in the old days."

"What do you think I do every night, Ki?" she replied.

# Chapter 2

When Ki had left, Jessie continued to ponder the invitation. She figured this Marquis must have an efficient network of spies and informants. Most very powerful men did; it paid, in the long run, to avoid surprise of any kind. Jessie tried to imagine what was his purpose in wanting to meet her so soon. Was it simple courtesy or curiosity? Or did it have more to do with the Starbuck enterprises than with herself? She had learned, over the long months since her father's death, that many men—many rich men—assumed that because she was a woman, her business interests would be easy marks. She had proved them wrong before, and would again if necessary.

None of these questions, however, changed her mind about going. She was decidedly interested in meeting the Marquis de Beaumont, this strange Frenchman about whom she had heard so many stories. He was either a genius or a madman, from what she could gather—or perhaps he was both, since those qualities often coexist in men. But now she had the chance to judge firsthand.

A porter returned her dress and she slipped into it. She brushed her golden-red hair until it shone. She was determined, as always, to show herself to good advantage at this first meeting. Her beauty, she realized, was an advantage she possessed in her dealings with men. While she would never consider cheapening herself through seduction for material gain, she knew how to make the best of social situations in which she could fully display her physical charms.

Satisfied that she looked her best, Jessie wrapped a lace shawl around her creamy shoulders and dropped a small hideaway gun—a Remington .41 over-and-under with ivory grips—into her silk purse. She met Ki on the front porch of the hotel. He had hired a carriage for her.

"The driver knows the best route to the house," Ki assured her. "There's a road that winds up and around the bluff. He tells me it's safe."

"Thanks, Ki." Jessie stepped into the rather battered brougham.

Ki said, "If you want me to go with you, just in case—"

"I'll be all right. You have your look around Augusta tonight. And relax."

"Until I know you are safely in your room, I cannot relax as you say."

Jessie smiled. She reached through the window of the carriage and took Ki's hand. "I'll be back by eleven. Don't *you* get into trouble while I'm away."

"Yes, ma'am," Ki drawled in imitation of the Circle Star ranch hands. They laughed, but the samurai could not rid himself of a sense of impending danger. He knew Jessie could handle herself in a scrape—and it was unlikely she'd encounter real trouble at the Marquis's house—yet he was reluctant to let her out of his sight. He waved as the carriage pulled away.

Jessie sat back, grateful for her friend's concern. She, too, felt that they had ridden into a potentially explosive situation—even though there was no outward sign of trouble in Augusta. She and Ki were, however, attuned to forces that operated beneath the surface. Their experiences on the

12

danger trail kept them constantly alert and poised for action in even the most seemingly innocuous situations. But the carriage ride was uneventful.

A bald Negro in evening clothes, his shoes polished to a gleaming shine, greeted Jessie at the front door. Inside, he took her wrap and led her through the vast, brightly lit foyer. Her eyes swept this way and that, taking in the spectacular sight: marble floors, elaborate chandeliers, sculptures and paintings lining the corridors, a wide winding staircase. She was no stranger to opulence, having traveled all over the world and visited some of the richest estates, hotels, and palaces, yet this display took her by surprise. Out here in the Badlands it was tough enough simply to survive, and most folks were grateful for a roof over their heads, period. But this—this castle in the midst of a newly founded frontier community—it didn't make sense. Who could afford it? And why would one build it out here in the Dakota Territory?

She followed the butler past a life-size statue of a naked Greek athlete with a spear. The figure recalled images from history books she had read at school, which told of a world far different from the one in which she lived. The finely muscled man was unclothed, and she marveled at the sculptor's skill in making the stone come to life as flesh. Was the ancient past really a simpler, purer time, when men lived by a true code of honor? That was what the history books had seemed to say. Were athletes and warriors of Greece closer to gods than were men today? Jessie had known many half-men in her life, men of violence and lies and greed. Were there no such men in times past? In this raw land in which she lived, men seemed closer to barbarians than to civilized nobles with a higher purpose than mere survival.

Jessie smiled to herself at this train of thought. She and Ki lived by their wits and their skill with weapons. She had killed her share of men—more than her share, perhaps. She did not like it, but it was a part of her life. Some might say she led a savage existence, but she was not one to judge others.

The heady opulence of her surroundings had tricked her senses for a moment. No, life in other times had its share of brutality and tragedy—as well as its moments of high achievement. But she believed that her own time would be looked back upon with an equal measure of disgust and respect. She and Ki and others were forging a new nation out here, making mistakes but achieving results. Still, as she thought of it, the whole business wearied her. Why not sell off Starbuck Enterprises and retire to a mansion like this and forget about the problems she faced every day? A tempting thought, but something she could not do....

"His Excellency the Marquis will meet you in the library, miss," the servant said.

Startled back to reality, Jessie composed herself. "Thank you," she said. He opened the tall, carved double doors and she stepped into the library.

The four walls were covered with bookshelves and paintings. A rich Persian rug stretched the length and width of the room. A writing desk stood in one corner, and elsewhere overstuffed chairs and reading lamps were scattered invitingly. Three men and one woman stood near a long mahogany table that served as a drinking bar, with bottles and glasses and flowers arranged neatly along its length.

"Thank you, Walter," said the smallest of the three men as he approached the newcomer. "Miss Starbuck, I am the Marquis de Beaumont." Erect, moving quickly yet gracefully, the man took her hand and put it to his lips. She felt the brush of his fine, dark mustache against her skin as he kissed the hand. "I am flattered that you have accepted my humble invitation."

"My pleasure, Marquis," she replied. Jessie felt his ice-blue eyes inspecting every inch of her body, appraising her curves and drinking in the soft sheen of her skin; she felt naked beneath his gaze. He smiled at her frankly.

"You are very beautiful. I had heard—" He waved a slender, manicured hand. "But I had not expected to find you quite so attractive!"

"Who, may I ask, told you about me?" Jessie was flattered but not won over by the man's obvious charms.

"Oh, beautiful women are so scarce in this vast, unpeopled land, are they not? I am perhaps attributing every description of every delightful female to you—and even then the superlatives are inadequate."

She didn't believe a word of his perfect, barely accented English. "That's quite nice," she said noncommittally. She was about to ask him about the messenger who had so rudely delivered the dinner invitation—had he described her to the Marquis?—when her host took her arm.

"Come, you must meet my wife and my other guests. This is quite an interesting party tonight." He guided her toward another man.

Jessie regarded this stranger with more than her usual curiosity. He stood ramrod-stiff, no more than average height, with sandy reddish-brown hair cropped short on his oversized head. His thick-lensed, wire-rimmed spectacles enlarged his piercing brown eyes, which seemed to miss nothing. His hand jerked up quickly to meet hers as a wide, toothy grin spread across his ruddy face. A thin mustache covered his upper lip, but it did not make him look any older than his mid-twenties. A perfectly tailored blue suit fit neatly over his lean but muscular frame.

"Miss Jessica Starbuck, may I present Mr. Theodore Roosevelt, a distinguished visitor from faraway New York. Mr. Roosevelt, Miss Starbuck."

Roosevelt's grip was firm but gentlemanly. Jessie shook his hand, immediately sensing a powerful friendliness and intelligence in this man. Despite his spectacles and pressed suit and fashionable Eastern sidewhiskers, there was nothing effete about him—unlike other dudes Jessie had encountered in her travels.

"Miss Starbuck," he said, flashing a mouthful of perfect white teeth, "it is the most pleasurable experience of my tour to meet you." Roosevelt bowed slightly, and Jessie thought he was going to kiss her slender hand as the Marquis had done. He did no such thing, merely bending and returning to his erect posture with a snap. His broad smile remained in place.

"Thank you, Mr. Roosevelt. That's a fine compliment; I doubt I can live up to that billing, though. Your tour can't have been too exciting."

"Oh, but it has been! This beautiful, alien country has already become a part of me—and I of it, I sincerely hope. I have been here less than a week, but already I love this land and the men who live here. It is an exciting venture, Miss Starbuck! The creation of a vital new nation still goes on—the Great Experiment, I like to call it." Roosevelt rocked back on his heels and puffed out his chest. "The very air, the big sky, the wild creatures—I have never breathed air so free, so alive. Where I come from, men live on top of one another in tenement houses on narrow, filthy streets. Nothing like this—nothing!"

The Marquis, who had hovered unobtrusively nearby, touched Jessie's arm with his cold, manicured hand. It startled her and she reluctantly turned her attention away from the Easterner.

"Miss Starbuck, I would like you to meet my wife, the former Augusta Heufer of New York." Jessie's gaze met that of a stunning, black-haired beauty with skin the color of polished ivory. Her pale, frigid eyes matched her husband's. Her slender neck and sculptured arms were bare except for a sparkling diamond necklace and a dangling

16

golden bracelet on her right wrist. She wore a long blue taffeta dress with a high waist and a frilly bodice that accented her small, perfect breasts.

The Marquis's wife nodded and lifted her arm languidly. Her soft white hand—which looked as though it had never touched anything rougher than an enameled hairbrush—felt like a flower in Jessie's own. Jessie felt no warmth from the woman; in fact, she sensed the opposite—a barely concealed hostility at the presence of another beautiful female in her home. As if the impressively outsized villa could not possibly accommodate them both.

Jessie nodded in return. "Thank you for inviting me," she said.

"His Excellency invited you," Augusta replied icily.

Ki felt uncomfortable staying in Augusta. He much preferred life on the Circle Star in West Texas—the easy discipline of ranch life, the open skies, the quiet times with Jessie and the crew. Cities and towns stifled Ki, caged his spirit. Night had descended; lights shone from the windows along the street. Raised planks enabled him to cross the muddy main avenue. *How do people live like this?* he wondered, always amazed at the poor conditions Americans would settle for. He supposed that since this was a young town, the people were working hard to better themselves. Why, then, the scent of decay he had noticed from the first? There was something wrong here. It made him worry about Jessie, on her way to dinner with the mysterious Marquis. Well, there was nothing to do right now but stay on his guard and gather whatever bits of information he could about the place.

For nearly an hour he walked the plank sidewalks in every direction he could, peering up and down the streets, watching the few people who were out. Nothing worth seeing, he decided. Not here in the streets. There was no better place to learn about a town's troubles than its biggest tavern, so Ki went to the Dog's Eye Saloon, a rudely constructed two-story structure that squatted on the western end of Augusta's main street.

Inside the dimly lit tavern he found his way to the bar, a long polished plank that lay, more or less solidly, on four tall, rough-carved posts. The place was roomier than it looked from the outside, with tables scattered over the floor and a staircase in the back that led to the upper floor. Ki estimated that there were thirty men in here, and he noticed two women who circulated among the men, serving drinks and sharing jokes. Some men laughed and shouted raucously, others played cards quietly around tables shrouded in smoke. Ki realized that the score of oil lamps hanging from the ceiling were not half enough to light the saloon brightly enough, even in the best of circumstances. He wondered when the place would burn down, and figured that it could happen anytime in such a carelessly maintained place.

He waited patiently for the bartender, who tended several customers before turning with narrowed eyes toward the stranger in the odd garb. A bear of a man with a shock of gray hair that stood straight up from his head, the barkeep placed his hands lightly on the bar. Ki sensed that few men dared cross this giant. The words *You've had enough!* probably rang with authority from this man's lips.

The hostility came through in his voice as he said to Ki, "There something I can do for you?"

Ki replied calmly, "A glass of your best beer. Please."

"I never seen you before around here."

"That is because I have never been here before. I arrived today."

"Generally we don't get your—kind, mister. My policy is I don't serve red niggers, but you is of a different breed."

"My father was an American," said Ki, his blood heating up. "My mother was Japanese. And I am thirsty for that beer."

18

The big man behind the bar studied Ki, not bothering to disguise the wish he had never seen this particular "yellow nigger."

"Cold beer will cost you ten cents, mister."

"As long as it costs every other man the same."

"High taxes is why." The big man fetched a bottle from the ice locker at the far end of the bar. He slid Ki's money into his pocket. "Nothin' personal, you understand," he said insincerely.

"No offense taken—yet," said Ki, as he uncorked the bottle and sampled the beer. It was cold, at least.

The big bartender kept his eyes fixed on Ki. He was sizing up the queer-looking stranger, still unsure how to treat the Oriental. Only a shout from another customer took him away, to Ki's relief. Ki preferred not to be the object of attention, though it was often difficult not to be stared at and questioned wherever he went throughout the West. Americans—at least those hardened souls who survived out here—were a suspicious lot, always cautious and wary of strangers. A man like Ki, who stood out in any crowd with his proud, erect bearing, yellow skin, and almond-shaped eyes, was bound to draw worried, sometimes hateful looks.

Ki surveyed the saloon, quietly observing the other patrons, watching the burly barkeep pour drinks and dispense private comments. He treated the two barmaids sternly but without abuse. Ki surmised that most of the men in the saloon were cattlemen, at least men who worked with cows, to judge from the smell of them. None appeared overly prosperous, though neither were they starving.

Two exceptions to the rule sat at one of the gambling tables. One was a dark, surly lump of a man with a broad Mexican face. The other was a wire-thin, hatchet-faced gunny decked out in a black suit and vest and a black, flat-crowned planter's hat with a wide brim. The pile of money at his elbow testified to his luck or skill at the game. It had been a good night for him so far. Ki saw that none of the

19

men at the table were smiling, not even the winner.

By the time Ki finished his beer, the game had broken up. One of the gamblers sat himself at a broken-down old pianoforte in a dusty corner and tinkled away his frustration. Ki ordered another drink. He would return to the hotel after this one. Nothing going on here. The big bartender was less unfriendly this time, but still distant, guarded. Ki paid with a silver cartwheel; the giant tavern owner examined it before making change. Ki had to admit the cold beer was good.

The thin, dark-faced gambler and the Mexican remained at their table. The prettier of the two barmaids, who, with her olive skin and shiny black hair, stood out like a flower in a pigsty, was talking to them. She wore a billowing red skirt and a low-cut white blouse that exposed her generous bosom to stunning effect. There was no mistaking the skinny man's interest in her obvious endowments. The other man spoke to her familiarly—in Spanish, Ki thought—but was more interested in his drink. What was the girl's relationship with these men, Ki wondered.

Other drinkers at the bar bent to their task. Most of them drank quietly, intent only on drowning whatever troubles plagued them, looking up only to signal the bartender for another.

But Ki, by training ever alert and curious, swept his gaze across the entire room. The only activity worthy of note was the discussion at the skinny man's table. He would have nothing to report to Jessie tonight. He knew, however, that she would have plenty to tell him. A first close-up look at the mysterious Marquis de Beaumont; Ki almost wished he had accompanied her to the dinner party. He didn't like the idea of her going alone. He knew she could take care of herself, but there was always a chance of something unexpected happening. He would never forgive himself if anything happened to her that he could have prevented.

His ruminations ended and his attention was diverted at

the sound of a woman's cry. "No, Niles!" It was the dark-skinned girl at the gunslick's table. The skinny man gripped her arm as she struggled to move away. The Mexican watched stoically, sipping his drink.

Ki's jaw tensed. The *bushido* code by which he was trained, which formed the basis of his life, called in equal measure for courage in battle and chivalry in love. A warrior could not stand by and watch a woman be insulted or threatened with physical harm. But Ki hesitated a moment. As always, he thought first of Jessie; his primary duty was to her, and he must not allow himself to be drawn into a fight that would endanger her or her interests.

No one else in the tavern seemed to notice the noisy confrontation. The man in the black suit did not raise his voice. He spoke to the girl through clenched teeth, his narrow, sharp face contorted in anger. His slender fingers dug deeper into her arm. She tossed her head in defiance, the mass of thick black hair whipping through the air. As she tried to pull away, the man yanked her toward him, forcing her into his lap.

Suddenly the burly saloon owner came out from behind the bar, wiping his hands and tossing the towel aside. "What the hell you doin', Korman? Let her go. Goddamm it, man, let her go!"

The man called Korman ignored the bigger man's warning. He pulled the young woman's face to his and kissed her hard. Holding her by the hair, he then pulled her head back and emitted a low, growling laugh. "Mind your own business, O'Hare. This bitch knows what she's getting into."

"By God, no man treats my girls that way," the bartender stormed.

"Back off," Korman warned him. "Here." He reached into his vest pocket and removed five silver dollars. "Take this for your trouble—and for an hour's rent on one of your dirty rooms upstairs."

21

By this time, none of the other patrons could ignore the scene that was ready to boil over. A few men made their way quietly to the door.

Ki eased himself erect and took a step toward the table just as O'Hare reached Korman and the girl. Then the Mexican entered the action. He stood up, pushing his chair away. As the chair clattered to the floor, he moved around his partner and the girl and faced the hulking bartender; O'Hare had at least ten inches on the Mexican, but the shorter man possessed long, powerful arms despite his squat build, and the black eyes flashed violently and fearlessly. He was itching for a fight.

Quietly, Ki said, "There is no need for trouble here."

"Who the hell are you?" Korman spat, retaining his hold on the girl.

"Stay out of this, stranger," O'Hare told Ki. "This has been coming on for a long time—it's between the Mex here and Korman and me." The giant was breathing heavily, clenching and unclenching his fists, ready to tear into the Mexican or Korman or both. But the Mexican acted fast, catching O'Hare off guard.

With a swift uppercut, the Mexican brought his balled fist into O'Hare's lower gut, doubling the big man over in pain and surprise. The Mexican grinned at Korman. O'Hare struggled for breath.

Ki stepped in to prevent the Mexican from dealing a death blow to the big saloonkeeper. He heard Korman say, "Take care of the Chinaman first, Jorge."

The black-suited gunman sat back with a crooked smile on his face and a secure grip on the girl, to watch the mayhem he had started. Ki caught a glimpse of the girl's tear-stained face. She was beautiful; she looked to be from south of the border, like Jorge, and Ki wondered what the hell she—and the mad-dog Mexican he now faced—were doing way up here in the godforsaken Dakota Territory. But

22

he had no time for philosophical considerations as he jumped to one side to avoid a side-arm blow aimed for his midsection. Ki landed with his feet well apart and firmly planted on the floor, his knees slightly flexed.

Raising his open hands, Ki maneuvered to his right to stand between the struggling O'Hare and the onrushing Mexican. Jorge, having regained his bearings, approached the samurai, swinging his big fists. Ki blocked the bricklike blows with quick, glancing forearms. A quizzical look fell on Jorge's broad face. The Mexican began to sweat. He was used to overwhelming his opponent with raw power, then pummeling through the weaker or smaller man's defenses. He had never seen a man fight like this strange, slant-eyed intruder.

Korman hissed, "Finish him, you son of a bitch!"

Jorge glanced toward the gambler. Ki saw his opportunity here, and landed his left foot in the Mexican's barrel chest and drove him back. Jorge's arms windmilled as he crashed backwards on the table and rolled to the floor. He came up, puffing wildly, angry as a blooded bull. He ignored Korman's flow of curses, which became more vehement with each passing second, and looked directly at Ki.

*"Hijo de puta!"* he breathed. "I must kill you now."

"No, Jorge!" It was the girl. Korman wrapped his hand around her mouth. She bit his palm, drawing blood. The skinny gunfighter slapped her face with the bloody hand. She just watched Jorge and Ki as if she hadn't felt a thing.

The Mexican crouched now and circled, having learned that a head-on assault would get him nowhere. He was still mystified at this yellow-skinned man in the rope-soled cotton slippers who moved like a cat—the only point of comparison being some Indian warriors he had seen, sleek and smooth and treacherous. Jorge grabbed for Ki's left arm, but the samurai wound free of the other's grasp. Jorge followed with a swift left that jabbed through Ki's defenses and found

23

its target: Ki's stomach. Pain stung the half-Japanese fighter, and he shifted his stance. He raised his left arm and, for a split second, stood stock-still.

Then, in a whirling motion, like a cyclone, he hopped forward on his right foot, his left leg half-raised, dropping that leg, chopping his arms up and down, and lifting his right leg to execute a smashing thrust to Jorge's jaw with the edge of his foot. He caught the Mexican under the chin and, with the power in his well-muscled leg, drove the foot up and in, snapping Jorge's head back.

Jorge's cry was choked off as his neck jerked back, and his stocky body followed. This time he landed on another table that collapsed under his weight.

Ki turned to O'Hare, who was just now regaining his breath and trying to stand upright. He went to the saloon-keeper's side, but the man waved him away and signaled to Ki to watch his own back. Before he could react properly, Ki felt a cold gun butt meet the base of his skull. He moved with the blow to lessen the impact, but the pain was intense, lowering a black curtain over his eyes.

Korman had tossed the girl aside and drawn his .44 Colt, a well-oiled revolver with carved walnut grips and the gun-sight filed down for an easier draw. In his skeletal fingers the weapon was a thing of monstrous beauty and precision. He waved the gun to warn off any others interested in joining the fray—but it was unnecessary, for the ranks of saloon patrons had drawn well back.

O'Hare muttered, "You black-hearted bastard, Korman."

"Shut your mouth, man, or I'll put a bullet in it," the gunslick growled.

The big man called Korman's bluff, lumbering toward him, saying, "You'd be doing me a favor, then. I hate this stinking town—and you and your boss up on the bluff. Kill me, you son of a bitch, and we'll meet in hell to settle it." He kept advancing in the face of the upraised revolver, his own eyes wild.

24

Korman's finger tightened on the trigger. He stood there coolly, daring O'Hare to come closer. But just as the tavern owner was almost upon him, the gunman felt a sharp, stinging blow to his wrist and watched the gun fly from his hand. Ki's follow-up blow was a swift, closed-hand thrust to Korman's chest.

The thin man staggered back, stunned, his mouth gaping. O'Hare moved in then, and Ki stepped away. The giant bartender reached out and grabbed Korman by his silk tie, pulling the man toward him.

"Scum like you don't belong in my place. Get out and stay out. And if I ever see you in here again—or anywheres near Olivia—I'll kill you!" With that he delivered a powerful slap to Korman's face that laid the skinny man's hawk nose sideways to the left.

The gunman howled, his dark eyes watering and blood pouring from the broken nose. "Jesus!" he shrieked. But O'Hare did not give him time to react. The bartender lifted Korman with one hand and carried him to the door. With a careless toss he deposited the gunny out in the muddy street.

Ki helped O'Hare lift the unconscious Mexican, Jorge, and send him in a heap after his friend. O'Hare went back and picked up Korman's unused Colt revolver. He looked at Ki. Then he heaved the weapon out the door, too.

Ki attended to the girl. She was sobbing, her face bloody from Korman's slap. Ki lifted her into a chair and carefully smoothed back her lustrous hair. He had heard O'Hare call her Olivia, and thought it was a beautiful name that suited her perfectly. The saloonkeeper came over with a pitcher of water and a clean towel. He put them on the table. Ki dipped one end of the towel in the water and gently wiped the girl's face. Her sobbing decreased. She looked up at her benefactor.

The other men in the saloon turned away and returned to their places at the various tables and at the bar. The man at the pianoforte resumed his out-of-tune ballad.

O'Hare said to Ki, "Mister, you saved my life. That was some fancy high-kickin'." There was no mistaking the big man's sincere appreciation. "Thanks for steppin' in. You all right, Olivia?"

The girl nodded, taking the towel from Ki. Her hands shook. "*Gracias,* Señor O'Hare. And *gracias* to you, Señor," she said, her eyes locked on Ki's.

Ki turned to O'Hare. "You know those men?"

"I should say I do. They're in here most every night, drinking and gambling. Couple of goddamned hired hands for that Marquis fellow up yonder in the big house. Nothing but trouble."

"I must thank you, Mr. O'Hare, for coming to my aid as well," Ki declared solemnly.

"Since you know my name, mister, and we done saved each other from the devil, what's your handle?"

"Ki." The two men shook hands, appraising each other anew.

"Funny name for a grown man," O'Hare mused. Then he said, "Sorry. No offense. Guess out there where you're from, they'd think our names was pretty funny."

"Men are men, wherever they may be, whatever their names."

"And some's pretty bad cases, like that Korman and his fat friend."

Ki was about to ask O'Hare for more information on the Marquis when Olivia stood, her face sad and noble despite her recent humiliation. She was beautiful even after her ordeal.

O'Hare said to her, "I meant what I said, Miss Olivia— if that skinny varmint comes near you again—"

"Please, Señor O'Hare, I will not trouble you anymore. Tonight I go. I will leave this place."

"Not on your life, gal," O'Hare protested. "You do good

work and I want you to stay. Tell her, Mr. Ki. No need to quit over this."

"I must," she said, averting her eyes from Ki's steady gaze. Her cheeks were flushed. She did not want to face him.

"Dadblame it, why? I just told you, gal—"

Olivia interrupted him. "I must. Niles—Señor Korman—will come back if I am here. And so will Jorge. Jorge is my brother," she said quietly.

# Chapter 3

Her host steered Jessie away from the haughty mistress of the chateau. The Marquis whispered, "My wife is unused to the presence of other beautiful women in her home. In this strange land, so far from family and friends, she lacks company appropriate to her station. Her father, you know, is a prominent banker in New York. It was difficult for her to give up the society in which she was raised and move with me—out here."

Jessie didn't think that was any excuse for the woman's rudeness. Madame de Beaumont's troubles ran deeper, Jessie surmised, than mere dissatisfaction with her present station. She sensed that the Marquis's wife would be unhappy wherever she was—in whatever company. And there was a measure of cruelty in her manner that Jessie would be careful not to encourage.

The Marquis said, "I want you to meet our other guest." He called to a man who stood apart from the others, "Mr. Hawthorne."

The man strode over to the Marquis. He was over six feet tall, with curly brown hair and a dark, lined face. His hazel eyes were clear and lively. Jessie noted with appreciation his broad shoulders and long, powerful arms. He wore an ill-fitting blue suit and seemed more than a bit uncomfortable in such formal clothes—and in such company, amid the splendor of the Frenchman's house. His gaze settled frankly on Jessie and he extended his large hand.

"Miss Jessica Starbuck, this is Mr. Dennis Hawthorne," Beaumont said. "Mr. Hawthorne is Mr. Roosevelt's guide." The Frenchman smiled, his eyes darting from Hawthorne to Jessie. He seemed to take personal delight in introducing the two, noting the big man's appreciative smile. This woman, he thought, would bring a smile to any man's face. And Hawthorne, the type of rugged frontiersman about whom the Marquis had read in the novels and histories of the American West, could not fail, even in his crude, unlettered way, to acknowledge her fresh beauty.

"A pleasure, ma'am," Hawthorne said, gently clasping her small hand.

"Mr. Hawthorne," Jessie replied. At the touch of his hand she felt a sensual spark. Looking into his eyes, which flashed now green, now brown, she thought she saw him wink at her. A friendly smile caused the deep lines of his weathered face to dance. Immediately she found herself liking this man. She wanted to get to know him better. Roosevelt's guide? What did that entail? she wondered.

The Easterner, stepping briskly, his arms swinging, joined them. The Marquis ordered a glass of wine for Jessie from the servant who hovered at her elbow.

Roosevelt, his winning grin lighting up his pale visage, said, "The wine is marvelous, Miss Starbuck. I do not drink to excess—for health reasons—but I do enjoy a fine glass of wine. The Marquis tells me he has imported an entire cellar of the finest French vintages."

Hawthorne said, "I stick to whiskey." He raised a finely

cut crystal glass and sipped the golden-brown fluid in it. "And I do drink to excess—sometimes—for health reasons." He and Roosevelt laughed, the latter pushing his spectacles to the bridge of his nose.

Jessie instinctively liked this pair of men, just as she instinctively held back from the Marquis and his wife. There was something odd about the group assembled for the dinner party. And again she wondered how the Marquis had known she was in town—and who his tough-looking messenger was.

The servant brought her a glass of fragrant white wine, which she tasted. It was cold and it slipped over her tongue deliciously. The Marquis's wife joined the group. "Marvelous," Jessie told the Marquis.

"A humble Bordeaux," he said diffidently, "but one of my favorites." He called for a toast, saluting his guests, wishing good health to all.

"Hear, hear," Roosevelt said, raising his glass. "And to you, Marquis, and to your lovely wife."

Augusta bowed her head slightly to the young Easterner and brought her glass to her lips. As she drank she looked at Jessie with barely concealed jealousy and suspicion in her cold blue eyes. Then her husband spoke again.

"And to the lovely Miss Starbuck," he saluted, avoiding his wife's baleful glare.

Jessie thanked the Marquis, still very curious at his seeming friendliness and openness. Were the reports she had heard about the trouble here in the Little Missouri Valley exaggerated? Or was the Marquis a very smooth operator? And what role did Augusta play in his schemes—if any? Perhaps the woman was too unhappy, living in the Badlands, far from her family and friends and social contacts, to care what he did. But somehow Jessie doubted that; the woman must have some power over the Marquis, if only through her influential and unquestionably wealthy father in New

31

York. Heufer was her maiden name. Where had Jessie heard that name before?

The black butler announced that dinner was served, and the party drifted into a vast dining room adjacent to the Marquis's splendid library. Jessie sat to Beaumont's right, beside Theodore Roosevelt; Augusta sat at her husband's left, beside the tall, handsome Dennis Hawthorne. Immediately a swarm of servants brought out the first course, a steaming consomme served in silver bowls. Likewise, the subsequent dishes, including a main course of pheasant, appeared before them rapidly and quietly. Several wines were poured with the meal, the Marquis recounting for his guests the origin of each. All were from France, all of the finest vintage, all delicious and appropriate. Jessie noted, however, that Dennis Hawthorne drank none of them, instead sticking stubbornly to his whiskey.

The Marquis asked Roosevelt about events back East, and the voluble New Yorker spoke at length about social and political events in his native city. His family—who maintained homes on East 57th Street in Manhattan and at Oyster Bay on Long Island—was an important and well-connected one. In fact, young Roosevelt was currently serving as a New York State assemblyman. And he regaled the party with tales of his exploits as a maverick legislator.

"One is supposed, as a new member of the august House, to be seen and not heard—like a well-mannered child. But, by the Almighty, that is certainly not the way I am!"

He favored them with a wide grin and went on, "I tell you, Albany is a cold town—except for the heat one generates oneself. I suppose—in fact I know—that my colleagues at first took me for a young bounder. Yet who can sit still for the shennanigans that go on? My initial weeks in the House were wasted—as were the other members'—by an incessant wrangling over the speakership. Those infernal Tammany Democrats—pardon my frankness, Madame de Beaumont and Miss Starbuck—have the Assembly by the—er, well, they have too much control. . . .

"Why, one day shortly after I arrived, one of the Tammany 'gentlemen,' a man much larger than myself, dared to insult my choice of clothing. There is nothing too petty, mind you. I'm afraid I had to park his backside on the floor of a local tavern, not once but three times. I do not say this boastfully, but as a matter of fact. I warned him that when he is in the presence of gentlemen, he must conduct himself like a gentleman. I bought him a beer and stood there as he drank it. He drank every drop and thanked me for it. He does not speak to me anymore, nor do his fellow Irish Democrats. But just as well—I have nothing to say to them, either!"

At twenty-three, Roosevelt was the youngest member of the State Assembly, but he had made his mark early and distinctly, fighting corruption and intransigence among members of the opposition party. A reform-minded Republican, he hadn't learned—and would likely never learn— to keep his mouth shut. A magna cum laude Harvard College graduate, son of Mittie and Theodore Roosevelt, Sr., young Teddy had survived a sickly childhood through a tough, self-imposed physical and mental regimen that expanded his quick mind and strengthened his wiry body. Always active, he hadn't relied on his family's wealth to get ahead in the world; he had grabbed what he could for himself, developing a talent for achievement through hard work. Of course, opportunities came more easily to a Roosevelt, but this young man sought out challenges himself, most often choosing the more difficult ones. His most recent conquest was a beautiful young woman named Alice Lee, who had become his bride less than a year ago.

"Do you know Commander Gorringe?" Roosevelt asked the Marquis.

"Yes. I met him on his recent visit. He bought some

33

property here, an abandoned army cantonment." The Marquis stated the fact as if it were of no consequence, but Jessie heard a note of resentment in his voice.

"Well," the young Easterner continued, "he told me about that trip when we met in New York City after the legislature had adjourned. I told him I had a notion to shoot a buffalo while there are still buffalo left to shoot."

Roosevelt laughed heartily, his somewhat high-pitched voice lending a boyish charm to his adventurous spirit. He went on, "The commander was supposed to return West. I was to join him. He decided, only several days ago, not to come after all. But by then I was determined. A bloody shame to cancel out. Pardon me again, ladies. My darling wife—who is expecting, you know—begged me to stay. As much as I hated to cross her, the poor dear, I simply could not turn back. By God, I'm determined to hunt buffalo, and nothing short of a flood or a cyclone will stop me!"

Obviously the New Yorker loved to talk and didn't shy away from talking about himself. Jessie was both amused and impressed. In some ways Roosevelt reminded her of her own father—or what he must have been like as a young man—ambitious, fearless, full of ideas, and willing to test those ideas against experience.

She wondered, though, if Roosevelt had ever faced a situation that required real physical courage. By the look of him, the man was a dude—not unlike other men she had encountered who talked a big game and then melted when they caught a whiff of blood, their own or someone else's. He had read all about the Wild West in books and had heard this Commander Gorringe's tales, but he had never been here before himself. At least he had made a good move in hiring Dennis Hawthorne. The tall guide, silent and wary as he sipped his whiskey, looked to be competent and tough, a no-nonsense man who wouldn't let the Easterner do anything foolish. Jessie guessed his age at about thirty, and she couldn't help glancing over at him again, observing the rugged leanness of him and the twinkle of humor in his hazel eyes.

The Marquis said, "You'll find nothing here if not adventure, my dear Mr. Roosevelt. That is why Madame and I live here, isn't it, Augusta?" His wife coldly acknowledged his statement; she had sat imperiously silent throughout the meal.

"I too enjoy a good hunt," the Frenchman continued. "However, I find even greater exhilaration in another form of adventure: making money. If you will pardon my boldness, I venture to say that I have laid the groundwork here to become one of the richest men in the world. A lofty ambition, perhaps, but not impossible." The Marquis spoke with almost frantic animation, his eyes alight as he scanned his guests' faces. For a moment his own face shone devilishly in the candlelight.

"I have plans. Yes. I see possibilities no other men see. It takes me mere seconds to evaluate and understand a situation that other men must puzzle over for hours or days. Cattle, for instance. That is my primary occupation right now. But that is only the beginning. I have invented a device that will revolutionize the whole meat-shipping industry, a device that will keep a railroad car cool—without ice—so that meat may be slaughtered a good distance from the marketplace, thus avoiding the cumbersomeness and expense of transporting live cattle over vast distances and losing market value through dehydration. The Northern Pacific Railroad has agreed to build a spur line to Augusta and to test my special railroad cars on the line to Chicago. I expect to have the first car built within a year!"

He smiled widely, toying with his wineglass. "Oh, yes, ideas. I love ideas. That is the legacy of my country. The French are great thinkers, Mr. Roosevelt. But mine is no mere philosophy; it is a plan of action."

"Admirable, Marquis," Roosevelt said with some hesitation. He regarded the Frenchman through squinted eyes, as if attempting to peer into the man's very soul.

Jessie could see that the New Yorker was uncertain as to how to phrase a proper reaction to this declaration. Hawthorne merely finished his drink.

"Another purpose of my trip is to explore the possibility of purchasing a ranch in the Little Missouri Valley," Roosevelt interjected. "I'd like to get into the cattle business myself."

"Well, it is not easy, sir," stated the Marquis.

"I'm sure I would be no competition for you, Marquis."

Then Jessie asked, "How many head do you run, Marquis. You know my family owns a small spread up north of here."

"Yes, I am aware of the Starbuck holdings," the Marquis said evenly, but with an unmistakable edge of hostility. "And we shall have to talk about that, Miss Starbuck. Right now I believe Augusta is exhausted, aren't you, my dear? We do not entertain very often. It is, of course, a strain on her."

The conversation wound down and the party rose from the table. Augusta excused herself and the host offered his guests some brandy, which they declined. Jessie, Roosevelt, and Hawthorne bade the Marquis good evening. Roosevelt offered Jessie a ride back to town.

The night was surprisingly cool, and she pulled her wrap securely over her bare shoulders as she stepped into the open wagon.

The three were silent for much of the short trip before Roosevelt said, "I'd be pleased if you would accompany us tomorrow, Miss Starbuck. Mr. Hawthorne and I are going to hunt those buffalo."

"I'd like to, but I planned to ride out to my property,

the Slash S, and look in on the foreman. Maybe another time."

Hawthorne said, "We'd like to have you, ma'am. We'll be riding north anyhow—your place will be right on our way. That is, we'd like to have you along if you can shoot. We don't want to be held up. We'll be in the saddle all day, and there's no telling when—or if—we'll run into a herd."

Jessie caught his implication. She was glad it was dark so the two men wouldn't see her face as it flushed angrily. "I assure you, Mr. Hawthorne, I can shoot—and I can ride as well as any man."

"Heavens," Roosevelt said, "I'm sure Mr. Hawthorne didn't mean—"

"I know just what he meant," Jessie insisted. "I believe I will accept your invitation, Mr. Roosevelt."

"Call me Teddy, all my friends do," the Easterner said. Again he smiled. Hawthorne looked straight ahead.

"Very well," she said. "My partner, Ki, will join us, too. He and I travel together." She addressed herself more to Hawthorne than to Roosevelt, hoping for a reaction from the big man. But she was disappointed. Hawthorne reined in the horses in front of her hotel. Roosevelt hopped down and offered his arm. "Thank you, Teddy," she said.

"My pleasure, ma'am," Roosevelt replied.

"And thank you, Mr. Hawthorne," she called to the driver.

"Think nothing of it, Miss Starbuck," the tall man said out of the side of his mouth.

She watched as they drove away to their own hotel, her anger subsiding. The nerve of Dennis Hawthorne! She swore silently to herself that she'd show him who could shoot!

O'Hare gave Ki a bottle of whiskey on the house. Ki accompanied the shaken Olivia to her room above the saloon, where she produced two glasses from a cabinet. Ki took a rickety chair and looked around the room as Olivia poured their drinks. There wasn't much to see. Other than the bed, the chair, and the small bedside cabinet, there were only a bureau and a crude wooden closet where, he supposed, she kept her dresses. She couldn't have many dresses, he thought. The cramped room was clean, though. He envisioned the girl sweeping assiduously on her day off, refusing to live in squalor despite the precarious nature of her life and her profession.

Olivia brought Ki his drink. She sat on the end of the bed nearest her guest. *"Muchas gracias,"* she said. "Señor Korman is an unpleasant man. I am glad you protected me from him. Jorge, too, is . . . unpleasant, even if he is my brother."

"You can't choose your brothers," said Ki sympathetically. "I couldn't stand by and do nothing. Men sometimes act like animals—and when they do, they must be taught a lesson."

"Señor Korman is not easy to teach. I do not think he learned anything but to hate you, Señor Ki."

Ki had a feeling she was right about that. Still, he wouldn't have done it differently. Men like Korman understand only force. He assumed Korman would come after him later. But, for now, the gunslick had a headache; he wouldn't bother anyone for the rest of tonight.

He asked Olivia, "What do you know about Korman?"

"Jorge says he is a big man, this Señor Korman. He works for the rich man in the big house. Jorge works for Señor Korman. So, Jorge says, my brother works for the rich man as well—and he will be rich himself one day, my brother boasts. My brother is not a good man, Señor Ki." Tears glistened in her soft brown eyes.

It hurt her to talk this way, and yet she wanted to get these troubles off her chest, Ki could see that. He reached out and put a comforting hand on her shoulder. She took a swallow of her whiskey.

"This Señor Korman comes in many times to the saloon," she continued. "He . . . likes me, he says. Señor O'Hare does not like Señor Korman and tells me to stay away from him. I try to stay away, but I cannot always. You see, my job— my work—it means I am with men many times."

Olivia spoke softly. She was ashamed of what she did for a living. Probably she said her prayers every night and confessed her sins to a priest when she had a chance. Probably she invoked the aid of the Blessed Virgin to take her away from all this. But for now, Olivia was stuck in Augusta, far from her home, selling whiskey and her luscious body.

"How did you and your brother come here?" Ki asked her.

"Our family, in what the *norteamericanos* call New Mexico, all of them died. It was a strange sickness brought to us by the soldiers. Many Indians died, as well as my people. Jorge and I were young. He took me away from there and we kept moving—all the time. A year ago we came here. I found this job. Jorge also found a job."

"You must not be ashamed, Olivia. You must survive. There will be a better day for you."

"I—I want to believe that," she said. The tears, one by one, rolled down her dark cheeks. She did not sob or cry out. She had learned to weep silently. With her sleeve she wiped the tears away.

"Tell me what you know about this rich man in his big house." Ki leaned forward in the chair. A lock of his black hair fell forward over his forehead. The girl's eyes ran over his lean, tightly coiled body. She had never seen a man like him before.

Olivia took a deep breath. "I know he possesses much land. This whole town is controlled from the big house. That's what Jorge says. And I know the people are afraid of him, some even say he is loco. I have only seen him a few times. He comes into town in a great carriage, sometimes with his woman. She is very beautiful. He is handsome, too, in his clean suit and large hat. He wears a gun at his belt and carries a big rifle. Usually there are many men with him, Señor Korman and others. I do not like the look in the rich man's eyes, nor his smile. I do not want him ever to see me. They say he likes young girls and that several from the town have been in his bed. The people here do not like him."

"How do you know what the people think of the Marquis?"

"The men talk in the saloon. Sometimes his own men talk. Like the men who work at the ranch. It is a big ranch and many men work there. They are vaqueros and they smell like cows. They drink very much and—" Her eyes fell. "Sometimes, Señor Ki, they pay me to lie with them. Most of the time they are drunk and they fall asleep. They talk in their sleep sometimes. I think the rich man treats his men badly."

"Why do they work for him, then?"

"Because he pays them well. And if they quit him, they cannot get other jobs in the town. The big house controls this town, as I said. Nothing happens here that he does not know about. He has spies, like my brother. The people are afraid of the Frenchman, but they want his money."

"So they allow him to run things his own way. What do other ranchers say about him?"

"They hate him," Olivia said bluntly. "The Frenchman wants to rule not only the town and his ranch, but the whole valley. He has said so. Many times he has tried to buy the other men's land. Other times he sends Señor Korman to talk to them. One man was killed."

"When did this happen?" Ki asked. Clark King, the Slash S foreman, had intimated as much to Jessie a few weeks ago. He wanted to know whatever details he could find out.

"Four weeks ago. He was one of the big ranchers, a

leader of those who do not like the Frenchman. He had turned down money, he would not give up his ranch. He was here long before the Frenchman came and built up his place. This man was not rich, but he was happy here. One night, after he had been in Señor O'Hare's saloon, he was shot on his way home. They did not find the body for many days."

"Who killed him?" said Ki.

Olivia looked at him, her lovely, heart-shaped face bleak with sorrow. "Señor Korman was here that night. He left soon after the rancher left. He and my brother. Jorge is like Korman's shadow. I fear for my brother, Señor Ki."

"Your brother keeps dangerous company."

"I tell him that, but he laughs at me. He says he'll be rich if he sticks with Señor Korman and the Frenchman."

*More likely he'll wind up dead before his time,* Ki thought. Jorge had chosen to die the moment he signed on with Korman and the Marquis, though he didn't know it. But the girl knew it, and that was part of her sorrow.

Ki finished his drink, and Olivia poured him another. She had sipped only a few drops of her own. Ki wanted the taste of whiskey tonight. And being with this girl was a pleasure he did not want to abandon just yet.

Olivia, curious about this strange man asked him, "Why did you come to Augusta, Señor Ki?"

"My employer holds some land to the north of here, along the river. She wished to inspect her property and establish contact with the man who runs it. We came from Texas, where we live."

"She? Your employer is a woman?"

"Yes. Her name is Jessica Starbuck. Her father was a rich man who had no sons. Only Jessie. He left her his fortune. I worked for him when he was alive. Now I work for his daughter."

"How old is his daughter?"

Ki couldn't help but smile. "She is about your age, Olivia. A year or two older, perhaps. And she is very beautiful."

"Oh," was all the girl could manage.

"You are very beautiful too," Ki said. He sat beside Olivia on her quilt-covered bed. His hand cupped her chin. "Very beautiful." She dropped her gaze from his. "Olivia—"

She looked up. Her dark brown eyes shone with emotion, still moist from her tears of a few moments ago. "Yes, Señor Ki?"

"No 'Señor.' Just Ki. Your eyes and your hair and your face, Olivia—you are very beautiful."

"Oh, Ki!" she whispered fiercely. She wrapped her arms around him, holding him, trying desperately to absorb some strength, some love from him. A total stranger until this moment, Ki had quickly captured a part of her as no other man ever had. She did not want to let him go.

The samurai had not had a woman in many weeks, yet he sensed that this one—beautiful and experienced and disappointed—was fragile. He would not force himself upon her. But he soon realized that it was not a question of force.

She lifted her mouth to his and drew him into a deep kiss. He felt her lips open, and their tongues met wetly. Olivia clung to him, pulling him closer, until he could feel her breasts against his own chest.

Ki broke free of her embrace and said quietly, "Olivia, you do not owe me this. A smile is thanks enough. You are a beautiful woman, but—"

"I want you to tell me how beautiful I am, Ki. I am not doing this to repay you. And you will not pay me. I want you, Ki. I need a man to love me, a true man and not a stinking cowboy. Please, Ki..."

Together they lay back on her bed, Ki slipping his arm

under her shoulders. Again they kissed, her tongue darting teasingly between his teeth. He held her face to his. She was in as much need as he, and he would not deny her—or himself. He felt her hands clutching at his back as her lips crushed against his. The fragrance was intoxicating: her skin, her jet-black hair, her warm breath. Even working in a saloon, she somehow overcame the offensive odors of smoke and liquor with her own freshness. And the taste of her—Ki plunged his tongue deep inside her mouth. Her breathing became heavier, her chest rising with delicious anticipation.

Ki lifted himself away, running his hand over her figure. Her blouse was cut low and wide, revealing a generous amount of her cleavage. As his fingers brushed across her breasts, Olivia shivered quietly, a current passing from her erect nipples throughout her entire body.

Olivia helped Ki with her clothes. First the blouse, then the skirt, then her shoes, then her corset and hose. Now she lay naked atop the bed. Her breasts were round, with large brown nipples that puckered invitingly; her belly was flat, her legs long and finely sculpted; and between her legs, the patch of soft black hair seemed to glisten in the diffused, soft light that came through the window. Ki admired her for a long time before touching her.

She reached for him and pulled him to her. Ki felt his own breath come sharply now as her fingers released the buttons of his pants. Then his erect shaft sprang free, only to be enveloped by her hand as she gently squeezed and stroked him.

Ki was determined not to rush, to take his time and make her do the same so as to prolong their pleasure, to take her mind off the pain and unpleasantness of the previous hours.

He slid down and took one of her nipples in his mouth and began sucking it. Olivia moaned in response. Ki sucked harder. The girl arched her back and cried out.

"Oh, Ki, don't!" she gasped. But he knew she meant the opposite of what she said. He gave his attention to her other breast, a soft mound that quivered under his loving ministrations. Again he trapped the nipple in his mouth and sucked it. Olivia had hold of his shoulders and tried to push him away—but she didn't try very hard.

"Ki, please . . . please . . ." she cried hoarsely.

The samurai said, "Olivia, I wish to make you forget your troubles. You are a beautiful woman who deserves to be loved—completely. I will give you much pleasure, if you allow me." His dark eyes met hers. She nodded silently, biting her lower lip. Ki kissed her again. Then he ran his lips down over her chin and neck, over her chest and belly, lingering below her navel, kissing her soft skin.

Ki repositioned himself and brought her silky legs over his shoulders. His tongue darted from his mouth like a serpent's, flicking gently over the moist folds of her sex. He began slowly, in a wide circle, tasting the pungent essence of her, then narrowed the circle and pressed his face closer to her. He penetrated her with his tongue and she called out his name. Ki lapped vigorously now, locating the swollen bud that sent ripples of uncontrollable desire through her. He pressed against the taut little nubbin with his tongue, and Olivia bucked; he licked at it, simultaneously using his fingers to part her love-lips. He slipped one finger, then two, inside her.

Olivia, unaccustomed to such surehandedness in bed, her body awash with new and somewhat scary sensations, reached down to clasp Ki's head. She felt his soft hair and gripped him hard.

"Ki—Ki—what are you doing? Mother of God, what—?"

Looking up, Ki could see her magnificent breasts rising and falling as she struggled for breath. He flicked his tongue harder and could feel the tension building within her. Olivia was silent many seconds, her hands pressing Ki's head. Then, suddenly, as he gave a final, darting wipe with his tongue, the girl came violently.

"Jesus! Jesus! Jesus!" she cried, her Spanish inflection making it a genuine prayer of ecstasy. Her legs squeezed Ki's head, as if she did not want him ever to stop. He cupped her buttocks, soft globes of flesh, and rocked with her as the orgasm flooded through her. And he could taste her flowing juices as she kept coming.

"*Ay, Dios!*" she whispered, "I never knew—never...Ki..."

She opened her legs and Ki, with one last flick of his skilled tongue, moved his body up on top of hers and kissed her long and hard, and she could taste her own love juices on his lips. She crushed her face to his and he could feel the tears as they fell from her eyes onto the bedclothes. With one quick movement, Olivia stripped Ki's white muslin shirt off, over his head, and went to work on his already unbuttoned pants.

As quickly as she could manage, she had him naked. She said, "Come, lie on top of me. I want to feel you against me." Her dusky, Mexican-accented words sent a shiver of arousal through Ki. He did as she asked.

Only the weak light from the window that fronted the street kept the small room from complete darkness. The air inside, cool when the lovers had first arrived, was now warm with their breath and the scent of sex. Olivia's skin shone darkly, and her eyes had a distant, unearthly focus.

"Ki, I've never known...no one ever made me feel this way."

"A man must give as much to his woman as she gives to him. It isn't difficult, Olivia, with a woman like you."

"Ki, love me. I want you, all of you. Please."

He put a finger to her lips. She smiled for the first time. She opened her legs, groping for his shaft. Finding it, she wrapped her fingers around its engorged length. For a tense few seconds she pumped it, and Ki held his breath. Then he lowered himself, letting her guide him inside her. As his weapon's tip met her wet nether lips, she sighed and pushed it in. She was ready for him, and took his entire length as it speared into her. The girl held on to his firm, muscular buttocks as he began thrusting, and lifted her legs into the air to give him easy passage.

Sweat broke out on Ki's forehead as he sent his sword deeper into her silken sheath. Olivia's hips rose beneath him, pumping with him. Her thighs locked around his as she writhed, meeting his strokes, which became more rapid. Her movements only aroused the samurai even more. He pulled his hot shaft out almost all the way until he heard her whimper, then plunged it back in, deeper than before. The girl moaned uncontrollably and worked her hips around and around. Ki impaled her, his thick length probing the depths of her honey-sweet sex, the animal in him taking over as they locked together even tighter.

"*Madre de Dios!*" Olivia cried. Ki felt her inner walls tighten around him. Once more he thrust himself into her fully.

Then, in a blinding flash, Ki came, spurting his hot essence deep into her. The girl, too, felt the spark and felt herself go liquid as she received his flood, which mingled with her own hot juices. Ki speared in and out of her as the impact of his orgasm diminished slowly. And Olivia did not want him to stop. But finally he was completely drained.

"I did not want it to stop," Olivia told him as she stroked his face. Both of them wore a thin sheen of perspiration in testimony to their passion. "Señor Ki, you are kind," she added lovingly.

Ki laughed softly, his eyes glistening. "Olivia, you are a young woman who has much to learn about life—and about men. But you will do well for yourself. I am not kinder than any man should be with a beautiful girl in his arms. You make it easy for me to love you."

Her breasts crushed against his chest as she held him tightly. He felt her dark, fragrant hair in his face and inhaled the still-innocent sensuality of her. Ki stayed with her until she fell asleep, and then he returned to his own hotel under the cover of darkness.

# Chapter 4

The party met for an early breakfast, then set off, riding north through the Little Missouri Valley. Roosevelt sat his saddle jauntily on a bay mare; he wore a brown leather coat and a black Stetson. In his saddle boot he carried a long-barreled Sharps .45-caliber rifle, which he had purchased in Augusta. Dennis Hawthorne rode at the point, his eyes cast down on the trail, looking for buffalo sign. Jessie studied the guide. In his fringed buckskins and floppy, low-crowned hat he certainly looked the part of a Badlands "character." He cradled a larger Sharps—a "big fifty"—in his powerful arms. He rode a glossy sorrel stallion with a white star splashed between its eyes and white stockings—a magnificent horse that matched its rider in height and strength.

Jessie herself wore a flannel shirt, a dark cotton jacket, and indigo-dyed denim pants; her mount, a sturdy black mare, carried her surefootedly through the gullies and ruts and ever-present underbrush. And Ki, as alert as he could be after his long night, rode at the rear with an eye on their backtrail. Despite the frigid morning air, he wore only his usual battered black leather vest over his cotton shirt and pants. Hatless, the samurai let the breeze catch his blue-black hair as he kneed his slender-legged gelding forward.

49

The four of them had exchanged few words since leaving Augusta, where Hawthorne had told them that, from his sense of the situation, there would be a lesser chance than he had originally expected for them to encounter a buffalo herd today. Therefore he recommended that they not take a wagon, as hunters normally did. If they were lucky, they could build a travois to carry the skin and meat back with them. Jessie was secretly glad, especially once the party got under way. The one time she had been with buffalo hunters, she had been disappointed and somewhat unnerved at their bloodlust—at the expense of the dumb, lumbering, somehow majestic animals of the open plain. Sickened, she had never thereafter enjoyed the idea of such slaughter. And besides, as Roosevelt had mentioned, there weren't that many buffalo left in these parts, thanks to the white man's efforts to exterminate them. Recently, according to Hawthorne, a Sioux tribe had returned to the Badlands and, with U.S. approval, killed off a herd of nearly ten thousand. The Indians couldn't have realized, Jessie thought, that the government policy of buffalo-killing would someday result in the elimination of the tribes themselves.

Looking around her at the beauty of this place, it was not difficult to think of more pleasant things. To the east, along the rolling river, rose tall, weather-scored buttes, yellow, rusty red, and chalk white. And beyond, on both sides of the Little Missouri, other, blunter buttes and hills of green and lavender faded into the distance. Where they rode, dense stands of oak and willow hugged the edge of the river; and beneath their horses' hooves grew a thick carpet of grass, interrupted occasionally by dark bogs and rock outcrops, and here and there wildflowers dotted the landscape. The sun rose higher, warming their progress and casting diminishing shadows among the ravines and rivulets they crossed.

A dry breeze was in their faces. Roosevelt spoke up with characteristic enthusiasm. "By God! This air will restore

50

me yet." He reined back to side with Jessie. "I tell you, Miss Starbuck, this is a treat for my lungs. You see, as a boy I was troubled with asthma—they thought for a while it could be consumption. Nothing so deadly—but uncomfortable, yes. I haven't breathed so freely in I don't know how long. A refreshing change from the stuffy, smoky halls of the Legislature, I can assure you."

The man's optimism and open nature were infectious. She said, "I'm glad it agrees with you. I must insist that you call me Jessie, though."

"By God! an interesting young woman. Very well—Jessie. I know so little about you and your charming Oriental companion. I feel at a positive disadvantage; I'm prone to talk so much about myself, and people are generally too polite to tell me to shut up. You're from West Texas, I gather."

"Yes. My father founded his ranch, the Circle Star, there. That's where I grew up."

She recounted the story of her father's life and death. Roosevelt listened to her tale in silence. When she came to the end of it he said quietly, "I remember reading about his murder in the newspapers. I'm so sorry, Jessie. He must have been a fine man."

Ahead, a long face of black rock marked a deep, twisting ravine. To Jessie it looked like a mournful reminder of the inexorable passage of time. How long had this scarred, chaotic land existed? Millions of years? What great cataclysm had slashed, with fire and water, across this isolated part of the earth? An awesome thought, yet when she was reminded of her father, all else seemed to shrink to insignificance before her memories.

"He *was* a fine man," Jessie said aloud. "He left me a powerful legacy. More than that, even, he left me memories that will never die."

Hawthorne had reined in and waited for Roosevelt, Jessie, and Ki to catch up with him. He said, "No sign more recent than two weeks, since the Sioux hunters were here. Used to be you could ride and find the damned shaggy brutes milling around by the hundreds. Just over that crest there's a big bottomland, plenty of grass—you could hear them from here. But now—" He shrugged. "We'll have to keep riding."

They broke for a cold lunch and watered the horses in a fast-running stream. By noon they were in the saddle again, riding north and west, covering the territory slowly, deliberately, as Hawthorne followed the faded trace of the once mighty herds. Along the trail they found the bleached bones of several buffalo that had either been shot and left or that had been consumed by coyotes and carrion birds. The grass in the bottomland of which Hawthorne had spoken grew nearly three feet high—plenty of nourishment for buffalo that were no longer here to eat it.

In the afternoon the country became more rugged. The Little Missouri meandered confusedly, forcing them to cross and recross it several times.

The river's banks were steep and treacherous, and when the party wasn't looking for a good place to ford, it was avoiding patches of quicksand and stands of blackthorn. It was slow going, but no one seemed to mind terribly, for they were in no hurry. Roosevelt seemed to savor the difficulty and danger of the expedition—for him all of this was new, an experience to write home about. In fact, he carried with him a writing book in which he occasionally jotted observations with a pencil. At lunchtime he had eaten distractedly, spending most of his time writing. He told Jessie he had written a book on the naval history of the War of 1812, and that he intended to write many more books in the years to come.

After one of the innumerable river crossings, Jessie rode up with Hawthorne. She had been wanting to talk with him all morning, but she felt strangely shy in his presence. Perhaps because of his size—which reminded her so much of her father—or because of his obviously taciturn nature. But she couldn't help thinking—knowing—that there was also a devilish sense of humor in the man. She remembered the glint in his eye last night, and his ready smile. As she brought her horse up next to his, she looked over at the guide, who sat his saddle ramrod-straight, his hatbrim obscuring his eyes. A familiar female tingle crept up her spine as she inspected his upright figure yet again.

"That's a marvelous piece of horseflesh," she said casually. "Where did you get him?"

"At an auction in Denver," Hawthorne said. He spat a wad of brown juice into the grass. "He was trained as a racehorse, but the owner couldn't control him—too much spirit for the track. But not too much spirit for me." His voice was edged with pride. It was apparent to Jessie that he took excellent care of this horse, and she liked that in him.

Hawthorne, for his part, liked her too. After all, the flaming red hair and flashing emerald eyes, the skin buffed and colored by sun and wind, the stunning figure that invited the touch of a man, the tight-fitting clothes that did little to conceal her physical endowments—what man could ignore such a filly?

Intensely private by nature, Hawthorne usually had little contact with women, except those of a certain type. Since he spent so little time in towns or cities, he was unschooled in the social graces—a lack he had felt keenly the night before at the Marquis's dinner party. It had angered and frustrated him, the gooey politeness and fancy get-up and strangely decorated drinking glasses. Roosevelt had fit right in; and so had Jessie, in her stunning long dress. Hawthorne, though, had felt like a mule in a corral of thoroughbreds. He didn't like the Marquis or his fancy, cold wife, but he was awed somewhat by their spectacular wealth and breeding. Hawthorne liked Roosevelt well enough—the son of a bitch talked too much, as Easterners usually did, but he had shown a good eye with his rifle and a readiness on the trail; he hadn't slowed up yet.

Ki was still a mystery to Hawthorne. He had met Jessie's half-Japanese, half-American friend only that morning; he had never seen anyone quite like this slender, yellow-skinned fellow. When they shook hands, the guide had felt Ki's friendliness, alertness, and strength. Hawthorne figured that if the man rode with Jessie, he must be all right. Which brought him back to Jessie . . .

He wondered what she'd think of him if she knew him—really knew him. At thirty, Dennis Hawthorne had lived among Indians and whites, in villages and cities, always alone, often in doubt of his next meal. A life on the cutting edge, never sure when he'd get the bullet in the back he fully expected. Not that he'd made a lot of enemies—but a man who lived as he did, on the trail, alone, could not expect to live to be an old man, no matter how careful he might be.

He never tired of the vast and empty Badlands, an aptly named stretch of territory like no other on earth. It had become his own through the years he had spent exploring it; and likewise it had claimed *him* as a part of itself. He scanned the harsh, unforgiving landscape for sign of the elusive bison.

Hawthorne looked over at Jessie and found her staring at him. She looked away with a faint smile. "Unlikely we'll find anything before sundown," he said. "Have to be looking for a good camp."

Now the sun slanted at them from the west, and the shadows of their horses lengthened.

Jessie said, "How do you rate our chances of finding any buffalo at all?"

"Slim," said Hawthorne. "I don't understand these folks' need to kill all those animals. Hell, just to kill them—that's what I don't get. Roosevelt ain't so bad. He wants one and ain't disinclined to eat it, rather than let the meat rot like most white folks. Most people, though, except the Indians, hunt buffalo for the so-called sport of it. I don't see how it's sport at all."

"It's worth the ride just to see this land," she said. "It's beautiful."

"And dangerous—like most beautiful things are."

Jessie glanced at the tall man. He was gazing straight ahead. She thought she caught a smile on his face before he leaned over to spit in the grass.

The Marquis de Beaumont stroked his trim mustaches. He sat in his library—the tall-windowed, high-ceilinged room lined with leatherbound books in several languages—behind a vast desk on which were scattered books and papers and maps and writing instruments. He bent again to scribble something, when his Negro butler announced Mr. Niles Korman. The Marquis pushed his high-backed leather chair away from the desk. "I'll see Mr. Korman," he said.

The skinny, narrow-beaked gunman limped into the library. He had donned a fresh black suit and knotted his tie neatly. He held his hat in his hands, nervously turning it through his fingers. A brace of Colt revolvers, holstered cross-draw style, rode on his slender hips. Across his nose lay a wide strip of white tape, and both eyes were swollen and black and blue. Korman's mouth was a jagged gash across his beaten face.

The Marquis repressed a smile as he asked, "Another alley fight, Monsieur?"

"No, goddamn it," Korman blazed. "Some chink at O'Hare's got smart while I was talking to Calderon's sister, Olivia. Thought he was doing her a favor by stepping in.

I would have killed him, boss—I wanted to. But I didn't. He—he got the jump on me—him and O'Hare ganged up together. O'Hare did this—" He pointed to his ruined nose. "He'll pay for it, too."

"I see," the Marquis said, his neat fingers forming a steeple below his chin. "You would have killed him, eh? Lucky for him you restrained yourself. Quite a sacrifice on your part." The Marquis stood up and came around to the front of his desk, leaning casually against the edge. "This 'chink,' as you call him—where did he come from?"

Korman said he didn't know, but he'd find out if the boss wanted.

"For a man with such a fearsome reputation, you can be terribly stupid, Monsieur." The Marquis took a cigar from a jeweled box and lit it. The blue smoke curled upward from his mouth. "I pay you a handsome salary to know exactly such things. Very well, then, I'll tell you who he is. His name is Ki, and he came to Augusta with Miss Jessica Starbuck. You do remember her, do you not?"

The girl in the bathtub at the Augusta Inn—he couldn't very easily forget her. But what was she doing with that yellow-skinned bastard? Korman was confused, and it showed on his battered face.

"Mon Dieu!" the Marquis exclaimed. "How fortunate I am that I do not have to depend on you alone for information. Korman, you tempt me sorely to discharge you right here and now. But I shan't. A cigar?" He held out the box, and Korman gingerly took one. The gunman struck a match on his boot heel. The Marquis continued, "Miss Starbuck accepted our invitation and dined with us last night—probably while you were wrestling on the barroom floor with your new friend. By the way, why didn't Calderon come to your aid?"

"Jorge got his lights put out early on. He wasn't no help to anybody. And that bitch of a sister of his—"

The Frenchman raised a pale hand. "Let us not insult

women, Korman. Where would we be without them, eh? Let us confine our remarks to the business at hand, which is pressing enough. Now, two things have come up. First, this Jessica Starbuck. I have been expecting her for many months. My sources in the East warned me about her. Very rich, very headstrong, and very beautiful. She owns the Slash S ranch north of here along the river—a prime piece of land, which I intend to appropriate. I'll buy it if I can, get it another way if I have to. I want you to keep a close eye on this young woman and her companion. That's not too much responsibility for you, is it, Monsieur?"

"No," Korman said, his eyes downcast. God, how his face hurt! Inside, he seethed with humiliation. He'd show that Chinaman—as well as the Marquis.

"A second, more pressing event has occurred," the Marquis went on. "Have you seen this week's *Badlands Chronicle?* Or do you know how to read?"

The contempt was thick in the Frenchman's voice. One thing he hated was to overestimate a man—and he was afraid he might have done just that with Niles Korman. But he'd give the man another chance to redeem himself. The Marquis took the most recent issue of that publication from his desk.

The *Badlands Chronicle,* a four-page tabloid, was published in Augusta by a young man named Paul Adams who had come West from Cleveland to work as a cowboy. His health and slight build had prevented him from succeeding in the saddle, but he had sensed a need in the infant community of Augusta for a newspaper and, with a small loan from the bank, had opened shop. He had been publishing for several months and had gained a reputation among the townspeople and the ranchers in the valley for fairness and accuracy. Most often, in reporting the ongoing conflict between the Marquis and the cattlemen, he had sided with the latter.

Now, in today's issue of the *Chronicle,* which the Marquis waved in his hand, Adams had printed a front-page editorial lambasting the Frenchman's high-handed tactics in consolidating his land holdings, implicating him in the recent murder of a prominent rancher. Earlier in the morning, the Marquis had read the piece, bile rising in his throat. It hadn't taken him long to decide that the young publisher had stepped out of bounds once and for all.

"The man must be taught a lesson, Korman," the Marquis said flatly. He stroked his fine mustaches. In his smoking jacket and silk pants, without a tie, the wealthy Frenchman looked the epitome of the man of leisure. But his abrupt manner and assured speech were those of a businessman who knew little of leisure. His consuming passions were simply money and power, and there was no rest for him until he had achieved what he set out to do.

"This Adams is nothing now, less than nothing," Beaumont went on. "A newspaper publisher, a troublemaker, a gnat. Of course, the people in the valley read this nonsense, some of them may even believe his lies. But this time he has gone too far. I want you to pay a visit to the *Chronicle,* Korman. Talk to Mr. Adams. Tell him I do not appreciate his lies. Persuade him to see the sense of my position. If he does not—well, there could be tragic consequences for him."

Korman managed a crooked smile. "I understand. I never liked that son of a bitch in the first place."

"Now this is nothing personal, Korman. Strictly business, as you Americans are fond of saying. Try to *persuade* him. He is enough of a *philosophe* to get the message. However, if you see that there is no persuading him, I must leave it to your impeccable judgment what to do then."

"I get what you're saying, Marquis," said the gunman. He flexed his nervous fingers. This was a job he could handle with ease. He looked forward to it. And from what he knew of Adams, the newspaperman wasn't one to knuckle under to "persuasion" or even money. He was a stubborn youngster with a ready tongue and a righteous disposition. Already Korman's broken nose didn't hurt so much.

"And this time, Monsieur," the Marquis warned him, "do not be so—what do you say?—messy. We do not want the entire town up in arms against us if we can avoid it. We have enough trouble with the rabble as it is. So be careful."

"I'll be careful, boss," Korman said. Would this pompous Frenchman ever give him credit for what he had done? Korman had worked for him for a long time now, and never yet made a serious mistake. The rancher's killing had not been handled as neatly as it could have been—but that was because Jorge had gotten carried away and forced Korman's hand. The Chinaman last night—well, that was a fluke and wouldn't happen again. The Marquis was so goddamned persnickety, like an old spinster who wouldn't tolerate a misplaced doily. Korman would show him. Already he had a plan to deal with the *Chronicle* editor.

"By the way, what do you intend to do about the Calderon girl?" the Marquis asked.

Korman looked at him quizzically. What did the Marquis care about a Mex whore? "I don't know," he said. "I guess I'll straighten her out."

"Good. I don't like my men to be unhappy. Women cause more accidents and trouble than all the newspapers put together. I should hate to see you hurt because of her. Perhaps she should take up residence in another town."

"I'll talk to her. After I finish with Adams."

"Good." The Marquis crumpled his copy of the *Chronicle* into a ball. "I never did like this newspaper. Perhaps I'll found my own. I don't expect we'll ever see another issue of the *Badlands Chronicle*, Monsieur."

"I don't expect so neither, boss," said Niles Korman.

The sun was a red ball hanging low in the sky. Jessie saw a magpie perched on the bleached ribs of a long-dead buf-

59

falo. Ki came up beside her as the party rode along a wide, dusty ravine. She could see that her companion was tired, though she knew he would never complain. He had been nearly silent all day long as they covered the rugged miles. He had been thinking of Olivia and the things she had told him.

Ki had learned the hard way to keep his counsel, just as he kept his weapons clean and ready for use. He was not one for talking—unlike the loquacious New York politician. He and Jessie often communicated without words, just a passing glance or inclination of the head. Quietly, now, he confided to Jessie his misgivings about the town of Augusta.

She said, "What could it be, Ki?" Having met the Frenchman, she saw that he had earned his notorious reputation by working subtly and quietly to achieve his ends. Some men had died, but who could pin the blame on this urbane, sophisticated, and charming Frenchman? Still, she was not naive; she knew that behind many a smiling mask a killer operated with deadly coolness. The Marquis was not one to be trusted or underestimated. Ki had his own theory.

"I believe the man Korman is eager to do some violence. After the beating he took last night, he will be desperate, having lost face in front of so many other men."

"Whatever he does has the Marquis's approval, I assume," Jessie said. "Even when he's not taking direct orders." She remembered the invitation Korman had delivered—the slavish yet clever cast to his close-set eyes.

"There is nothing we can do about it out here," Ki said.

"We won't be back to Augusta for two days at the soonest." She shook her head, the red-gold tresses beneath her hat catching the ruddy rays of the dying sun. "I hope you're wrong, but I don't think you are," she said. Just then, Dennis Hawthorne halted the party. "Look!" he called, pointing ahead as he crested the upslope of the ravine.

60

The others followed the guide, Roosevelt first, Jessie and Ki behind him. On the grass lay a cake of fresh buffalo dung; leading from it were tracks. Hawthorne pointed to the spoor. "He was here not more than an hour ago, maybe a lot less."

Roosevelt jumped in his saddle. "By Godfrey! Are you sure, Hawthorne?"

"Just one, judging by the tracks. A bull," the guide said.

Jessie felt her heart jump. It was exciting, after all, to come close. The thrill of the hunt rose within her. Hawthorne advised the party to check their weapons. Jessie unsheathed her Weatherby, a big-bore English rifle that her father had brought back to the Circle Star. It was one of the finest long-distance weapons ever manufactured, with an almost flat trajectory.

Ki strung his long bow and uncapped his *ebira* quiver, where he carried a dozen sharp-tipped hunting arrows that he had made himself. Shunning firearms in most situations, Ki was an expert bowman, and it was one of his favorite weapons.

Hawthorne's .50-caliber Sharps was the gun preferred for years by serious buffalo hunters, Roosevelt's .45 version an older weapon best carried by inexperienced hunters like the New Yorker. Roosevelt stuck close behind the guide for the next half hour as Hawthorne followed the fresh tracks.

Suddenly, unexpectedly, in the gathering dusk, the party heard a snort and the crackle of underbrush. Ten yards ahead, a shaggy-headed bull bison charged out and galloped across a shallow-banked coulee, disappearing behind a giant rock outcropping to their right.

"That's him!" whispered Roosevelt urgently, his rifle at his shoulder, vainly at the ready.

Hawthorne spurred ahead, splashing through the stream, and the others galloped after him. They saw the buffalo about a quarter-mile ahead. Despite his awkward bulk, the animal lumbered up the face of a tall butte. Leaping agilely to the ridge, the old bison turned and looked back at his pursuers as they closed the distance. He shook his great head and ran off.

"Sly old man," Hawthorne breathed. He gathered the party around him. "He's dealt with hunters before. Generally, buffalo ain't that smart. But this one has survived. He may run all night, or we could catch him before the hour's up. Not much light left. What do you want to do?"

"We must pursue him," Roosevelt said definitely, his blood rising at an opportunity so near.

Jessie and Ki agreed, for the Easterner's sake. No point in giving up now, while there was some daylight left.

They were on the edge of a stretch of prairie, a vast grassland that seemed to stretch for countless miles. Beyond the grass were more hills that hugged the land tenaciously and held many secrets in the gullies and little valleys they formed. As Hawthorne urged his horse ahead, the others increased their pace and went up over the bluff where the bull had last been seen, then across the flat top and down the other side, sloping toward the river. They rode hard to a stand of junipers, where the guide halted them. He dismounted and told them to do the same.

"Best to go on foot from here on. Keep low, the grass is tall, stick to the bushes and trees. He's somewhere between us and the water. We'll fan out and close in on him. Mr. Roosevelt, you'll get the first shot, so don't hesitate. If necessary, though, I'll kill him myself. I don't want to risk anybody getting hurt. Understood?"

The party agreed. Hawthorne glanced at Ki's long, taut bow and quiver. "That's the quiet way, all right," he commented. "One of those arrows in the right place can stop a bull buffalo as sure as a Sharps. Where'd you learn how to use that thing?"

"In my own country," Ki replied. "I was taught by a master."

Hawthorne directed them to spread out. They did, crouching low, and advanced, signaling to keep themselves aware of each other's position. The tall grass ended about four hundred yards from the river's edge. Roosevelt blundered out into the open, he was moving so fast.

And there he saw the old bull, water dripping from its muzzle, its shaggy flanks heaving, staring directly at him. It was no more than three hundred yards from him. He raised his rifle.

Hawthorne reached the clearing next, followed by Jessie, on Roosevelt's right, and Ki on Jessie's right. The animal took no notice of any of them; its old eyes were riveted to the bespectacled Easterner. Jessie saw Roosevelt steady his weapon, showing no signs of faltering. Then she heard a loud snort and turned to see the buffalo wheel, run in a tight circle, then charge straight at Roosevelt.

"Fire, man!" Hawthorne yelled.

At two hundred fifty yards, Roosevelt squeezed the trigger. There was a loud crack and dust spat up around the animal's hooves. Roosevelt had misjudged, aiming too low. Then Hawthorne's long-barreled weapon discharged.

The buffalo, distracted by the sound of that gun, hauled to a stop, wheeled again, and cut across the clearing away from Hawthorne. Jessie's gun was raised, but she did not fire. She watched the big bull point its horns toward the river and gallop several hundred yards. Angrily it tossed its dark-maned head and circled back, bellowing its frustration in a surprisingly weak-sounding roar. Roosevelt fired again, but he didn't come close, and the old bison turned and galloped away haughtily.

"Drat!" Roosevelt exclaimed. "I ruined it!"

Hawthorne, who was impressed with Roosevelt's nerve in the face of the charging animal, said, "Hell, no. I missed too. These damned things ain't easy shooting, except when they're all together in a herd. That's how the so-called great buffalo hunters racked up all the numbers, by firing into herds of thousands. Hell, you can't miss like that. Don't feel too bad, Mr. Roosevelt. Maybe we'll get another try tomorrow."

Jessie added, "You just have to aim a bit higher. If you'd like, you can use my Weatherby tomorrow. It's better for long-range shooting."

"Thanks, both of you. If we happen across the old terror tomorrow, I'll give him what-for." The grin spread across his face, all those teeth on display. "Mr. Ki, you didn't loose a single arrow. I daresay you should have given it a try."

The sky was gray, the sun hovering at the edge of the horizon and splashing red across the tortured, time-scarred land, as they remounted and rode on in search of a campsite.

Jessie fell in beside Dennis Hawthorne. The guide had handled the situation very professionally, she thought. He had given the Easterner the lead at the appropriate time and backed him up with firepower, encouraged him to try again. She wanted to talk to Hawthorne about something else, though.

"That's a fine rifle," he said, before she could speak. "I'd think twice about loaning it out, even to Mr. Roosevelt. I will say he's got a head on his shoulders, for a dude."

"Are we going after the buffalo tomorrow?" she asked. "I'm thinking that I'd better head out for the Slash S. Ki seems to think there's trouble brewing in the valley. And I trust his feelings about things like this."

"Ever since the Frenchman came, there's been trouble a-brewing in these parts," said Hawthorne. "Especially among the independent cattlemen. Seems the big man wants to be the biggest man, doesn't want competition. He can't see why some of these other men want to hang on to their hardscrabble ranches. It might be a tough life, but what they got is theirs."

"You don't like the Marquis much," she said.

"Not much. I don't mind drinking his whiskey—it's good stuff. And I don't turn down his business. But as to liking the man—no. He's out to grab it all for himself. It's not right."

"Is there any organized opposition in town, or in the valley?"

"The Marquis never gives 'em enough time to *get* organized. That rancher who died recently—was murdered, that is—he was talking with the other cattlemen, trying to get them to band together and fight the Frenchman. Look what happened to him. That's as close as anybody's come."

Ki had told Jessie about the slain rancher and Olivia's conclusions as to who had done the killing.

"When you say the Marquis is out to grab it all for himself, what do you mean by *all?*" she asked him.

"I mean, ma'am, just what I say. That man wants near as much of the blamed Dakota Territory as he can swallow. That includes every inch of ground we've covered today and just as much south and east of Augusta. He aims to build himself an empire, all right, crown himself king. All these crazy schemes—and some of them ain't so crazy— like the cooled cars for transporting beef, that's to make him rich. The land, that'll keep him rich and be something to pass on to his kids. If he has any. That wife of his is as cold as an icicle."

Jessie's laugh rang out in the heavy dusk.

"I know a good spot to set up camp," Hawthorne said, and he led them to a scooped-out section of grassland between the river and a towering bank of blackened scoria.

Jessie built a fire and cooked a simple dinner and boiled a large pot of black coffee. Hawthorne poured a generous dollop of whiskey into his coffee and offered the bottle to anyone who wanted some. Roosevelt took him up on the offer and spiked his coffee likewise. After his meal the Easterner pulled his notebook from a saddlebag and began to record the events of the day. He wrote furiously, in a small hand, squinting in the poor light of the campfire.

Ki went immediately to sleep, rolled in a woolen blanket far from the fire. Jessie sat beside Hawthorne, who rolled and smoked a cigarette. She was tempted to ask him for some tobacco; a good smoke would help relax her. But she refrained. Instead she watched Hawthorne as he smoked, his eyes closed, his legs crossed like an Indian's.

Something about this man attracted her—his self-knowledge, his skill on the trail and with a rifle, his easy yet authoritative manner, his piercing green-brown eyes. She liked him, though she did not feel close to him. He was a private individual, not part of the crowd. He did not make it easy to get close.

She threw out the dregs of her coffee and cleaned the cup. Spreading her bedroll apart from Ki's, she lay down and looked up at the glassy black sky. Unsettled but unafraid, she reviewed the events of the past two days, gazing all the while at the glittering pinprick stars and the sliver of moon. Pulling her soogan up to her chin, Jessie was glad she had Dennis Hawthorne on her side if it came to challenging the Marquis with guns—and a part of her was convinced that it would indeed come to that. She smelled a killing fever in Augusta.

# Chapter 5

In the morning the party swung northeast and rode onto Starbuck land, the Slash S. It took them more than an hour to reach the ranch house and outbuildings. During that time, Jessie attempted to put aside the unappetizing thoughts that had troubled her all night. She hadn't slept well, for two reasons: a vision of the Little Missouri Valley engulfed in a range war, and her growing interest in the handsome hunting guide, Dennis Hawthorne.

*Leave it to a woman to be a bundle of contradictions*, Jessie kidded herself with a faint smile. Even though she traveled in a world of men—at all times as an equal—she often felt the distinctly feminine urge to let *them* take care of business and let her stay home with her cows and her cooking and, one day, her children. She reminded herself that she had come a long way on the vengeance trail; most folks would consider Alex Starbuck's memory avenged many times over. But that part of her which remained unconquerably her father's daughter would have no part of giving up. Now, with rare exceptions, her life was the trail, was the Starbuck empire, was the life of a leader and a fighter. That was why she told herself she shouldn't shrink at the thought of a fight with the Marquis or whoever else might challenge her for her birthright. It was legally and rightfully hers, this vast network of wealth, and she was determined to fight for it—to the death if necessary.

She relaxed in her saddle. Ki saw the results of this inner debate on her face, which was now more composed, determined. He had watched her worry all night and into the morning, and he was glad she had come to some conclusion for herself. It was part of what the samurai had tried to teach her—inner peace makes the warrior stronger in warfare.

Hawthorne and Roosevelt rode behind, talking quietly about the previous day's hunt. The New Yorker pumped his guide for analysis and advice concerning the buffalo chase. Next time, Roosevelt wanted to get it right. Hawthorne cautioned him that the likelihood of encountering more bison was remote at best.

Jessie and Ki talked of the Slash S. "I can see why my father bought this land," she said. "It is beautiful." The rolling hills were still lushly green, and coulees veined the land; occasional bluffs and steep cutbanks scored the spread, and a few head of Starbuck cattle found haven in these hiding places. They'd have to be disturbed at roundup time, she realized. "Look, you can see mountains, far off to your left."

The nameless, low-slung range was just visible from where they were. "How many acres are yours, Jessie?" Ki asked.

She calculated briefly in her head. "Only five hundred acres. I'm sure my dad planned to acquire more, once the herd began to multiply. He figured a five- to ten-thousand-acre spread would be profitable, once the means to ship the beef became available, which shouldn't be too long now."

Ki said, "Olivia Calderon told me an interesting story about your friend the Marquis."

"He is *not* my friend, Ki, just because I accepted a dinner invitation," she said with some heat.

68

"It was a joke, Jessie," he said with a wide smile. "One of the Frenchman's money-making schemes," he went on, "is a cooled railroad car to transport beef from the Dakota Territory on the Northern Pacific. An ingenious idea, if he can carry it off."

"He told us about it at dinner," said Jessie. "And he *will* carry it off. I also get the impression he'll charge his fellow ranchers—whoever is left—a hefty fee to use his service. Meat buyers will love it, though. Anything to make their jobs easier."

"Jessie, when we get back to town, I want to look in on Olivia. She was afraid when I left her. Her brother doesn't help matters—being tied in with Niles Korman and the Marquis."

"You've taken a liking to this girl?" Jessie asked him with a grin.

Ki didn't answer, and Jessie smiled, recognizing the silence for what it meant; her friend had apparently taken more than a mere liking to the Mexican woman. She knew how women could be instantly and intensely attracted to him—his exotic eyes, his clean skin, his strong chin. She only hoped Olivia's involvement with Ki would not put the girl in more danger than she could handle.

"I'm anxious to get back to town, too," Jessie said. "As long as all is well here at the Slash S. I'd like to see the Marquis de Beaumont again and ask him some questions."

Ahead stood the modest ranch house, a lone man-made sentry amid the variegated landscape of the Badlands, a thin ribbon of white smoke spilling from its chimney. A small barn, a good-sized corral, a bunkhouse, and an outhouse—these were the only other structures, and they flanked the main house. All the buildings were freshly painted and well maintained so that, despite their insignificant size, they testified to the pride and discipline of the occupants.

A lone hand, a very young fellow whom Jessie guessed

to be about seventeen, saw the four riders approaching and dashed into the house. He came out armed with an ancient, brass-mounted Enfield, followed by an older man in his mid-thirties, toting a more up-to-date .44-caliber Henry repeating rifle. The two rifles were casually pointed at the riders as they approached.

"Hullo the house!" Jessie shouted at fifty yards. "Friendly party here. Are you Mr. Clark King?"

The foreman said he was, squinting at the strangers, wondering how they knew him. And a woman leading them—it dawned on him then who she was. "Miss Starbuck?"

"That's me," Jessie announced. She dismounted a few yards from King and the boy—who regarded her with open-mouthed amazement. He'd never seen anything quite like Jessica Starbuck in all his seventeen years.

"Mighty proud to meet you, ma'am, after all this time. Sure is a surprise, your coming here. Guess you got my last letter."

Jessie said she had. Then she introduced the others in her party. King shook their hands and quickly gathered that this was a blue-ribbon inspection visit. He scratched his chin. His face was gaunt but dimpled at the chin, his hair a wire-stiff shock of salt and pepper; he wore a blue workshirt and black pants above a pair of labor-scuffed leather boots.

"Well, I'll be d—" King shot a glance at the boy. "This here is my little brother, Randolph, Miss Starbuck. Say hello to the lady, boy." He had to push the youngster toward Jessie. Plainly, the kid was fatally smitten with her. His face turned pink as he grasped her hand. Jessie deflected his embarrassment by introducing him to the men.

King said, "Wish to heck I'd of known you was coming, ma'am. I'd of had Georgie whip up something special for you and the gentlemen."

A woman emerged from the house. Blonde and prettier than most ranch wives, Mrs. King was hugely pregnant. She wore an apron over her long kitchen dress and was wiping her hands on a frayed towel.

Jessie said, "Sorry to drop in on your unexpectedly, Mrs. King. We were riding in the area and I thought I'd just come along."

"Call me Georgie," the woman said. She opened her arms in a friendly gesture, welcoming Jessie and the others inside. "That's for Georgia, the state of my birth. So far away now—the name's all the connection with it I got left."

Jessie followed the woman into the house. The inside was as neat as the exterior. There wasn't much room; a stove and dining table dominated half of the house, and the other half was divided into two small chambers, each with a bed. Georgie had enough chairs to seat the visitors and her husband around the table. She quickly ground some coffee and put a fresh pot on the stove. An aroma of baking bread pervaded the room. Hawthorne rolled and lit a cigarette.

King said, "Don't have any whiskey to offer you, or I would. Don't get a chance to drink much myself—and we don't have folks dropping by, neither."

"From the looks of things, you're pretty busy, Mr. King," Jessie commented. "The place appears to be in good hands."

"Thank you, ma'am. I—that is we, Georgie and me and my brother—appreciate the chance to work the place. Your father, Mr. Starbuck, hired me, and I was proud to work for him. We're all really sorry he passed the way he did. He was a fine man."

"He always knew exactly what he was doing, and he did the right thing in signing you on, Mr. King, I can see that. What would you say if I were to make you half-owner of the Slash S and finance the purchase of three hundred head in the spring?" She had made up her mind about this man

71

quickly—she liked him. And she wanted to reward him for his loyalty and good work; this place was worth it. He stammered his thanks, looking from Jessie to his wife and back, blinking as if trying to awaken himself from a dream.

Then he said, "There's only one thing, Miss Starbuck—"

"Call me Jessie, please. We're partners now."

"I kinda like that, Miss—er, Jessie. But, like I said in my reports to your office in Texas, you might want to think twice about keeping this place. The valley ain't a peaceful place these days. There's a lot of unrest among the ranching men—and in town. This French fella, the Marquis, he's stirring things up quite a bit."

"What Clark is saying," Georgie put in, "is that this Frenchman is trying to buy out all the independent cattlemen and take over the whole valley for himself and rule it on his own say-so. And we don't like him. We don't want his money. We want to stay here, as long as you'll have us."

"We've heard as much from others—including the Marquis himself," Jessie said. "As far as I'm concerned, the Slash S is here to stay."

Roosevelt who, with Hawthorne and Ki, had been listening all this time, couldn't help but inject himself into the discussion. "I say, I think this attitude is bully. Jessie, if you're so sure you can keep this operation thriving, you might have another bidder than the Marquis. The more I see of the country hereabouts, the more I like it; I may want to invest in a ranch of my own while I'm at it. I'm not having any luck with the buffalo."

King regarded the Easterner with a questioning look. He said, "Don't know as it's the best time to be jumping into the cattle business in this valley."

"That's just the point, my good man!" Roosevelt showed his teeth in all their abundant whiteness. "The greater the risk, often the higher the return. The Marquis is by-gum

72

certain what he wants, and you are, too, and I like the feel of this land."

Georgie poured coffee all around. The black brew smelled and tasted delicious after the hard morning's ride.

His impatience at sitting still beginning to show, Hawthorne said, "Might be nice to have a look around the spread."

"I'm all for that," Jessie said, having regained her energy and enthusiasm with the coffee and the good company. She was anxious to have a closer look at this bit of prime Badlands property, and to question King in more detail.

Clark King saddled his horse, leaving the disappointed young Randolph to moon over Jessie and help his aunt with supper. The boy grudgingly accepted the unmasculine chore and watched the five ride away.

For several hours the foreman led Jessie, Ki, Roosevelt, and Hawthorne on a far-ranging tour of the Slash S, reaffirming Jessie's commitment to the beautiful parcel her father had purchased years ago. She could see why he had bought the land; the grass and water were plentiful, the sky big and open, the expanse of the land seemingly endless. By gum— as Roosevelt put it—she'd fight for it if she had to.

"When do you plan to get to the fall roundup?" Jessie inquired of King at one point.

"I've already set a date—in two weeks—but it won't be easy to hire men this year. The French fella is talking it down—or his boys are. Us valley ranchers'll have to lend one another a hand, and that'll take us all more time than usual. Lot of the able hands in town are taking the rich man's money *not* to work this season."

"Damnation!" Jessie cursed. Then, when she had cooled down a bit, she said, "We'll get it done somehow."

The others in the party were equally impressed with the ranch. Roosevelt plied King with questions concerning land management and cattle breeding and feed and expenses and the like, absorbing as much information as possible in such

73

a limited time. His prodigious memory would lose none of these facts, as his intense gaze took in impressions of the land like a camera.

Dennis Hawthorne, glad to be out of the house and in his saddle, tried hard to keep his eyes off Jessie. He welcomed the distraction of the tour. But somehow he found himself almost unable to ignore her sensual presence.

The burning in his brain and the bulge in his pants reminded him painfully that he hadn't been with a woman for months. And with a woman like this—well, he hadn't ever. He reined in his horse and fell behind the other riders. *Damn it,* he cursed silently. *Start thinking too much of women and you'll lose your edge—and you can't afford that. Don't waste your time wanting something you'll likely never get.*

The party returned to the ranch house in time to enjoy Georgie King's sumptuous supper right from the oven, including a thick beef stew, buttered biscuits, and, for dessert, an apple pandowdy drowning in fresh cream. More coffee followed that, leaving hosts and visitors speechless and sated. The sun went down on them, and the visitors made a move to leave. Georgie tried to persuade them to stay, but Jessie refused with thanks.

"You're going to sleep in your own bed, Georgie—we're not turning you out in your condition. By the way," Jessie asked, "when's the baby due?"

"Almost any day now," the proud woman answered. "This will be our first, Clark's and mine."

King directed them to a convenient campsite less than a mile from the ranch house, but repeated his offer of shelter.

Roosevelt said, "Do me good to spend another night out of doors. Good for my lungs, you know."

"And we want to get back to town first thing tomorrow, Clark," Jessie added. "I want to amend the papers to make us partners—and I have a few things to ask the Frenchman. Good nig it and thank you. I'll be back in a couple of days and we'll make arrangements for the roundup. Take care of Georgie."

Ki took the first watch, and Jessie could hear Roosevelt snoring as she pulled her soogan up to her chin. Her mind was racing, and she tried to put all the pieces together, all the things she had learned—many of them unsettling—about the situation here in the Little Missouri Valley. "Some folks call it the Little Misery," King had told her with a wry smile. She could see why, especially given the Marquis's drive for control at all costs.

What troubled her most was the increasing evidence of turmoil and the possibility of violence as the independent valley ranchers stood up against the Frenchman and his gun hands. Her stake in the conflict was as large as the other cattlemen's. And, tired as she was after many months of fighting to maintain control over her vast legacy, she wouldn't hesitate to defend the Slash S and the Kings by whatever means necessary—that is, if the Marquis's men dared challenge her directly. As Jessie closed her eyes to try to coax herself to sleep, she couldn't shake the vision of impending bloodshed. . . .

Suddenly she sat bolt upright, her converted .38 Colt upraised and cocked. A shadowy figure approached silently. Jessie steadied her aim and prepared to fire. Then she heard the figure speak.

"It's me, Jessie—Dennis Hawthorne."

Relieved, but somewhat unnerved by her tense reaction, she brought the gun down. "What are you doing up?" she asked.

"Couldn't sleep—Teddy's snoring, for one thing," he said with a chuckle. "And I guess I think too much sometimes. Wondering what's going to happen here in the valley. Doesn't look too sweet for King and the others."

"That's exactly what I was thinking," Jessie admitted.

75

Hawthorne sat on the cold ground next to her. She saw his eyes sparkle in the pale moonlight. His curly hair fell over his ears, and he hunched his wide shoulders as he crossed his legs Indian-style. "I can't help worrying," she said. "Not that it does any good."

Hawthorne spat toward the dead campfire. "Seems that's how most folks around here spend their time—worrying."

"Shouldn't be that way," she mused. She felt his eyes on her in the darkness. "What's your stake in this, Dennis? You're not a cattleman. You don't have to stick around and get shot at—if it comes to that."

"Oh, it'll come to that. It has already. There'll be more lead, more corpses before it's all over. That fellow in the big house wants it all, Jessie. I've known him for over a year. He hired me when he first came here, and I rode with him all over the valley, saw him fall in love with it—like I've seen other people do. But it was something different with him. I don't know how to explain it—sort of crazy, the way he talked as if it was all his by rights. Once I heard him say he was kin to some of those old French kings. Said he could have the throne if he cared to go back and fight for it. He sets his mind on something and he doesn't care who gets hurt, as long as he gets what he wants. I didn't figure, though, that he'd stir up so much trouble here, once he saw how tough some of these ranchers are. I took him for a dude at first. Then, once when we were out hunting, he showed me he could handle a gun—pretty impressive. He shot a grizzly at ten yards, didn't flinch. I'll never forget that."

Jessie was curious to know more. "Where does he get his money?"

"From what I hear," Hawthorne said, "his wife has most of the money. Her old man is a big banker back in New York. Friend of the Roosevelt family, as a matter of fact. An old German family—Heufer. Anyhow, the Marquis must have put on a good show to attract the girl and her father, and he succeeded. Now he's living mostly on money from his wife's father's outfit, from what I hear. Guess that's why he named the town after her—her money built it."

"What about these gunnies he keeps? Like this fellow Korman that Ki ran into. Where does he come from?"

"Who knows? Word gets around that a rich man is spreading cash like butter, buying land, building a town—men like Korman flock in like buzzards. If the rich man is smart, like the Marquis, he'll put these men to work for him, instead of fighting against them. Like I told you, the man in the big house has brains, Jessie. Don't underestimate him."

"I won't," she told him. "I just want to know his next move."

"Hard to tell. Could be he's wondering the same thing about you."

Jessie laughed softly. "He wouldn't like your telling me all this."

"I gave up caring what he thinks a long time ago. I don't like the man, Jessie. He doesn't belong in this valley—in this territory, for that matter. If it comes to fighting him, I will. I—I'll be pleased and honored to side with you."

She sensed that it wasn't easy for the guide to talk to her like this, frankly and personally. She was happy he had come over to see her. What would his arms feel like around her? She imagined kissing him, and wondered what he tasted like. Her eyes were now more accustomed to the darkness, and she could see his rugged features clearly. He was gazing directly at her, a faint smile creasing his face.

She said, "God, Dennis, how can we stop it before it blows up in our faces? I don't want to fight if I don't have to."

"Best way is to go right to the source, the Frenchman. You get him to limit his ambitions and stay in that big house of his—and that will solve a lot of problems. But, like I've been telling you, he's more than a little crazy. Won't listen to reason."

Jessie shook her head. "I still don't understand, Dennis, why you stay here. If what you say is true, there's no future here for you."

He sidled closer to her and said, "The only answer I can give you is that I don't belong anyplace else, Jessie. I'm not like you, with kin and a family place and a name to live up to. My people weren't nothing but sodbusters in western Kansas—and not too successful at that. The old man died when I was young, and I drifted off and got captured by some Cheyenne Indians. Lived with them for a long time, till I figured I really didn't belong with them either. Been wandering since then—odd jobs, a lot of miles. Got as far as San Francisco once, and stayed there for a while till I got sick of city living. Kept to the trail most of the time since then. That's why I like the Badlands—you can go for days without seeing a human soul."

"You're not lonely?" Jessie asked.

"Sure, I'm lonely. But I'd rather live that way than trapped in some town with people breathing down my neck all the time. The Badlands is a friendlier place, the people are spread out more, and I don't get in anybody's way."

"You mean nobody gets in your way," she said, prodding him.

"Damn it, Jessie, I mean exactly what I say," he blazed. Then, seeing the twinkle in her night-dark eyes, he lightened up. "You know how to rile me, that's for sure."

Around them the night grew cooler and quieter. The only sound they heard—apart from Teddy Roosevelt's sonorous snoring—was a distant owl hooting.

She said, "I don't aim to rile you, Dennis. But I kind of like it when you get angry. You can't be lonely and angry at the same time."

"For a woman, you're awful smart," Hawthorne said.

This time Jessie reacted angrily. "What do you mean, 'for a woman'?"

"You're not so hard to rile yourself, Miss Jessie Starbuck."

"Shut up. Come here. Kiss me, Dennis."

The man didn't need to be told twice. He came to her and took her in his powerful arms, crushing her to himself. Their lips met in a wet, fiery collision of passion and clung hotly. *This is a cure for loneliness, all right,* he thought.

Jessie snaked her arms around to grasp his well-muscled back. She closed her eyes and drank in the kiss. She was not disappointed in his taste. A lightningbolt exploded in her brain and she could feel the tears rolling down her face. He felt them too and, pulling away, looked at her.

"What's wrong, Jessie?" he asked, concern scoring his voice.

"Oh, hell, Dennis, it's nothing really. I just can't take my mind off what's happening here. I think of those nice people, the Kings, and all the others in the valley—and I wish there were some way to avoid trouble."

He kissed her again, then wiped away the tears. "For God's sake, quit worrying about it, woman. I have to take my watch in a few hours. Let's not waste time fussing over things we can't change."

"Yes, Dennis," she whispered hoarsely. "Help me forget. Make me feel nothing but you, only you. Love me, Dennis—I need you."

The blanket fell from her as she rose to her knees and pulled Hawthorne to her. The big man eased himself down beside her on the hard ground. Again they kissed, their tongues fighting, his strong hand tangled in her flowing hair. His hot breath mingled with hers, and their bodies pressed together as they lay there. For a long moment there was nothing but the touch of their lips and the rapidly building anticipation within them.

Hawthorne's hand explored the luscious shape of her

body, blazing a trail from her neck, over her bosom and flat stomach, to the nest of passion between her legs. He rubbed her firm mound of Venus through the fabric of her pants as she clutched at his shoulders. She felt his curly hair against her face and whispered in his ear, "Help me take them off, Dennis."

The guide lifted himself on one elbow and, with his free hand, unbuttoned the fly of her denims. He pulled the soo-gan up to shield her bare flesh from the night. Slowly he caressed her—the softness of her belly, the firmness of her thighs, the mysterious wet folds that parted before his thick fingers. He rubbed her there, coaxing a groan from her. She grabbed his wrist as if to stop him, but he resisted, contin-uing to rub her nether lips and flicking his work-roughened finger over the soft button of her sex.

"Jesus, Dennis!" she cried.

His touch was so manly, so authoritative, so pleasing that Jessie didn't want him to stop, yet she couldn't take so much, so soon. She gritted her teeth as a wave of sweet lust crashed over her. Then she felt his hand move up under her shirt, groping for her breasts. She unbuttoned the shirt as he cupped a taut globe in his hand and squeezed it gently. Jessie pulled his head down and he took her nipple between his lips. With lips, then teeth, he grazed the erect nipple, sending electric tingles of desire throughout her body.

Half undressed, with only the cover of the thin blanket, she felt completely naked and vulnerable in the hands of this rugged stranger. And yet, in a sense, he was not a stranger at all. It was as if she had known him forever. She opened her mouth soundlessly.

"Jessie, I want to make you feel good. I haven't ever known a woman like you." He buried his face in the curve of her neck, flicking his tongue over her skin. He lifted his mouth to her ear. "You're so beautiful. I want you, Jessie."

"Yes," she replied, breathless.

Her hands rested on his broad chest. She played with the buttons on his shirt, slowly releasing them until the shirt fell open. Her fingers slid through the thick, matted hair on his chest, grazing his nipples, her fingernails scratching his skin. "Where did you get these scars?" she asked as she felt the imperfectly healed wounds on his muscled stomach and side.

Hawthorne gave a gravelly laugh. "I picked 'em up here and there. That one in my gut was a Comanche arrow that near killed me, down in the Staked Plains. A renegade band I stumbled on by mistake. Never made that mistake again."

He fumbled with his belt, finally freeing the buckle, then he undid the buttons on his own pants. The pressure in his groin was mounting. He felt her hand beside his; she undid the last button and reached inside. Hawthorne gasped, "Christ, girl!"

Jessie's fingers closed around his enormous, hardening shaft. Blood rushed to his member as she kneaded it, and it grew stiffer.

"Is that all yours?" she asked in amazement.

"The Comanche never got close to taking that away from me." His answer was choked off by Jessie's playful squeeze. Her slender fingers slipped under his sack and she tickled him there. "Stop that," he commanded gutturally. But she continued teasing him.

"I'm meaner than any Comanche," she joked.

"You're going to kill me, for a fact," he said.

"But not before you put this thing inside me, Dennis." She reached down and took him in both hands, massaging the tumescent sword to its full length. His breath came in short gasps as she pulled at it more quickly, and a drop of fluid appeared at the bulbous head. Hawthorne, not to be outdone, put his finger to work at the moistening lips that guarded her love nest. He rubbed her there, then inserted the finger slowly.

This rough teasing continued as they worked themselves into a frenzy of passion. But neither of them could hold out much longer. Hawthorne slid an arm under her back. She urged him on top of her, keeping a firm grasp on his member. Hawthorne let her guide him inside. Her tightness was exquisitely painful at first, but he thrust harder until she had taken almost his entire length. Jessie moaned as she tried to take him in. He was so big, so hard, that it nearly took her breath away. She opened her legs wider to allow him smoother access to her innermost regions; she felt his length to the very core of her being and tried hard not to cry out. She arched her back to meet his strong thrust, and she knew she had taken all of him.

"Give it to me, Dennis," she demanded through clenched teeth.

Hawthorne obeyed, working his hot sword in and out of her smooth sheath. She bucked beneath him, locking her knees against his strong legs. *Damn these clothes!* he thought, wishing they had stripped. But the moment was too urgent, they couldn't stop now. His scrotum tingled and tightened at the base of his manhood, and he pulled out slowly until only the tip was touching the soft, wet lips.

Jessie felt suddenly empty, and sighed, "Come back. Put it back in me."

With a powerful thrust he filled her up again. Dizzy with the heat of desire, she pulled his face to hers. She kissed him hard, pressing her teeth against his, battling his tongue, tasting him as he continued to pound her. God, it was like nothing else in the world, to have a big man inside her, to forget everything else but the sweet release, to give back to him as much as she got! She wished it would never end.

"Please, Dennis . . . don't stop . . . please . . ."

He didn't. He increased his rhythm as she lifted her pelvis and opened herself to him completely.

They rocked together in the primeval love dance, sweat beading on their faces and heat increasing in their loins.

Jessie came once, then again and again. She muffled her cries of indescribable delight; her brain felt like a hot-air balloon rising above the clouds and bursting among the stars. And below, in the cauldron of her sex, Hawthorne continued to stir the boiling juices with his powerful staff until she felt her legs melt.

The guide felt her contractions around his engorged manhood as it slid in and out of the silken cave. His heart jumped to his throat then as he fought his own impending climax. But it was no good. The volcanic eruption spilled forth. From head to spine he experienced the blinding jolt of sexual release, and all was liquid in the darkness between them.

Collapsing into her arms, spent, Hawthorne slipped his tongue into her ear. Jessie jerked away with a weak laugh. "For God's sake, Dennis, stop it," she said.

"Can't stop," said Hawthorne. "Don't want to stop."

"You're a big brute. You must weigh twice as much as I do—and you're crushing me." She planted her hands on his chest and pushed. He gave way, slowly pulling out of her, and rolled over beside her. Jessie gasped as they finally uncoupled.

"You can't get rid of me now," he told her.

"I don't want to. You may be a brute, but you're *my* brute."

"Thanks a lot," he said.

"You better go get some sleep over in your own bedroll, mister. You want to be fresh for your watch."

"Sleep? I'll never sleep again—not after that." He pulled his pants up and buttoned them. Then he kissed her again.

Jessie said, "That was nice, Dennis." She ran her hand tenderly across his shoulder. "Good night."

"Good night, Jessie," Hawthorne replied. He returned to his bedroll on the other side of the cold fire.

For Jessie, sleep came after a while—a troubled sleep in which she dreamed of Ki and Dennis and herself fighting for their lives against an unseen but powerful foe.

83

# Chapter 6

Jessie wanted to see for herself. Upon her arrival in Augusta at noon, she had returned to her hotel room to clean up, but Dennis Hawthorne came to her as soon as he heard the news about young Paul Adams and the *Chronicle*. Ki had foreseen something like this. Two nights ago the newspaperman had been attacked in his office and killed, the office itself ransacked. Jessie went with Hawthorne and Ki to the *Chronicle* offices—or what remained of them.

It wasn't a pretty sight; the interior of the small frame building was a chaotic nightmare of destruction, and the printing press was broken into a hundred pieces, with paper and ink and furniture scattered all over the floor. It looked as if a Kansas twister had hit the place.

"I never met the man," Jessie murmured, "but I think I would have liked him." She felt rage building within herself. There was no doubt in her mind as to who had caused this horrible destruction—but how to prove it? And should she act now to avenge this senseless act?

Ki and Hawthorne inspected the office thoroughly, looking for any kind of solid clue to link this murder raid to its source. Both of them had a good idea who was behind the act. But they could find nothing that would stand up as evidence in a court of law.

Ki said, "I don't like the spirits that inhabit this place. I can smell blood not yet spilled, I can hear the cries of the dead not yet dead. There will be a battle, and many will die."

Hawthorne looked at the samurai strangely. Having lived all his life close to the wild land, he didn't possess a mystical bone in his body—even after his years with the Cheyenne. And yet, somehow, he believed Ki's prophecy without question.

He said, "Jessie, it's about time for another powwow with that damned Beaumont, don't you think?"

Jessie agreed. "I hate to jump to any conclusions, but I'll be damned if this doesn't point to him and his hired gunmen. I figure I'd better get invited to dinner again."

"Don't go alone," Hawthorne advised.

Jessie smiled painfully. "Teddy could use another free meal, too. He can escort me. We'd better talk to him about this."

"Jessie, maybe we'd better contact the territorial authorities," said Ki.

She thought about that for a moment. "Not yet," she concluded. "I want the Marquis de Beaumont to provide us with more evidence. I'm sure he has his own contacts. If he hasn't, he's stupid—and I don't think that's how he works. Besides, we don't know for sure that it was our rich French friend who actually did this. He'll have his tracks covered if he did."

"You've got to be careful, damn it," Hawthorne put in vehemently, concern written on his handsome, weathered face. He had a stake in Jessie's safety himself now. "Beaumont is a smooth bastard."

"I'm always careful, Dennis," she assured him. Turning to Ki, she said, "See what you can find out from Miss Calderon. This has the smell of that man Korman and her brother."

They left the newspaper offices feeling downcast, frustrated, furious. Hawthorne led them to Roosevelt's room, where they found the Easterner at a makeshift desk, scribbling on a long sheet of foolscap. His glasses were perched precariously on the bridge of his nose as he bent, squinting, to his task. He looked up and gave Jessie and the others a wide grin.

"I've just given my dear wife an account of our latest adventure. When she reads this, she will be well acquainted with all of you, my friends." His jocularity ebbed, however, when he saw the intent look on Jessie's face. "What is it?" he asked, putting down his pen.

Jessie related the news and told of the visit to the remains of the *Chronicle* offices. Roosevelt listened in stony silence. When she had finished, his fist came down on the desk with a loud thump.

"By the Almighty! Who is responsible for this dastardly deed?"

"No way to be sure until we see the Marquis again," said Jessie.

"You think Beaumont may have something to do with this?" the New Yorker asked, incredulous.

"Apparently the *Chronicle* had come down on the side of the independent ranchers in the valley. The young publisher, Mr. Adams, ran an editorial a few days ago, condemning the Marquis for criminal tactics in his effort to buy out—or drive out—these rival cattlemen. He sure won't be publishing anything more against the Marquis."

"The young man is dead, you say?" Roosevelt shook his head grimly. "That is a violation of the First Amendment, to say nothing of capital murder. It bears out what your foreman, Mr. King, told us yesterday. Nothing short of outrageous, I call it!"

"We must speak to the Marquis," Jessie went on. "Do you think you and I could arrange to see him tonight?"

"Nothing could be simpler, my dear Jessie. I shall write him immediately and request an invitation to dinner. He will be interested, I'm sure, in hearing of our adventures over the past two days. And we shall give him an earful, as they say." He began writing on a fresh piece of paper.

Hawthorne said to Jessie, "I still don't like it. Who knows what the bastard will do if he thinks you might go against him."

"If he does anything, I doubt it will be tonight, and I doubt he would dare threaten me—or Teddy."

She remembered how polite and solicitous the Marquis had been on their first meeting. It *was* hard for her to imagine that this cultivated, rich foreigner was capable of such raw tactics as murder to gain land, power, or more wealth. Upon close examination, it just didn't make sense. But she had encountered bottomless greed before; the cartel that had destroyed her father was the embodiment of such destructive, dangerous greed. So she couldn't rule it out in the case of the Marquis. Nor could she forget King's story of the murdered rancher. If times were bad in the Little Missouri Valley, all fingers pointed to the Marquis for making them so. Would he listen to straight talk from Jessie and Roosevelt? Well, there was only one way to find out—and she'd find out tonight.

Ki returned to O'Hare's place that night. This time the saloonkeeper greeted him like an old friend. But the samurai was not in the mood for a friendly chat. He ordered a beer and asked for Olivia.

"Something's wrong with that little gal," O'Hare confided. "She ain't been herself the last couple of days—since you dealt with Niles Korman and her brother Jorge. She's been askin' after you, but I weren't able to tell her where you were. Where were you?"

Ki told O'Hare about the hunting trip and the tour of the

Slash S property. The bartender said, "I know young King. Nice fellow. Quiet, always pays his bills, never drinks too much—maybe one or two whiskeys every few weeks. A good man."

"What kind of man was Paul Adams?" Ki asked directly.

An angry cloud passed over O'Hare's face. "He was a good man, too. A hard-working man, not out for trouble. But he had a fault—couldn't help tellin' the truth as he saw it. Had no use for that fancy-ass Frenchman on the hill, neither."

The big man put an elbow on the bar and leaned closer to Ki. His shaggy gray eyebrows were drawn together as he said, "He was found dead yesterday morning, his skull bashed in and three bullet holes clean through the heart. I don't have no doubts who done it—or had it done. It stinks of fancy French perfume to me." He spat in disgust, hitting a spittoon behind the bar with a clang. "I liked Adams. Clean youngster from the East, somethin' wrong with his lungs. Came out to the territory for his health. Goddamn it." These last syllables O'Hare growled with contempt.

"Did you hear anything that night?" Ki asked him.

"Nothin'. I must've been sound asleep upstairs." He gestured with a beefy hand toward his living quarters. "Once I drop off, can't nothin' wake me but a bomb. I heard about it in the morning, like most everybody else. Makes me sick to think about it. There ain't no official law 'round here, so nothin's been done to catch the killers. Need a posse, I say—get some of the men together and ride to the house. Hang the man."

Ki said nothing. If the people in town knew the Marquis had ordered the murder of Paul Adams, what was stopping them from doing just as O'Hare was suggesting? The Marquis was loathed by all, yet he had some unspoken power over Augusta and its citizens. After all, it was his town, named after his wife, financed by him. And his chateau was defended by armed henchmen like Niles Korman and Jorge Calderon and who knew how many others. Easier for these people to grumble and complain about the Marquis than to ride against him and flirt with death.

Just then, Ki saw Olivia enter the saloon. She was carrying a canvas bag and wearing a shawl around her head. She didn't see Ki until she came right up to him. Startled, the girl cast down her eyes and spoke to O'Hare.

"Señor, I am leaving. I do not wish to stay here and work for you any longer. *Muchas gracias* for everything you have done for me. You have been very kind. Goodbye."

"Wait a minute, gal," O'Hare protested.

"Olivia, you cannot leave," Ki said.

She looked at both of them, her dark eyes pools of sorrow and fear.

"My life is in danger if I stay," said Olivia. "My brother has told me so. I do not wish to stay."

"Where is your brother?" asked Ki.

"I do not know. And I do not care." The girl's voice trembled and she would not meet Ki's eyes. "I must go away from here."

"Gal, you've got friends here," O'Hare said. "Mr. Ki and me, among others. For Christ's sake, we'll help you. I don't very much like that brother of yours—and I don't want to see you get hurt any."

"*Gracias,* but—"

"No buts about it," the saloonkeeper stated. "You've got a room here and you know it. Stay here, missy."

Ki saw that O'Hare had a heart and really liked this girl. Perhaps the gruff Irishman was the only man who had ever been good to her. For whatever reason, Ki saw that she listened to him.

"I want to talk to you, Olivia," Ki said. "Let's go to your room. Please hear what I have to say."

Finally the girl looked up at Ki directly. "I will stay—

if you and Señor O'Hare wish it. But my brother told me to go."

"Come," said Ki. He took the canvas bag from her and led her upstairs. Inside her room she sat on the bed, tossing the shawl to the floor.

With Ki's encouragement, the girl pulled herself together enough to tell him coherently what had transpired over the past two days. She dried her eyes and said, "He told me I was to stay away from you. He knows we went to bed together. He slapped me—told me Señor Korman did not like me sleeping with a Chinaman. Then he told me it would be best if I left town and never came back, because Señor Korman is very angry with me. Jorge promised to send me money, wherever I went. But I don't think he would; he has never given me anything—even when it was just the two of us, he would drink up all the money he made. I had to work, too, so that we could survive." Her beautiful dark face was gaunt with grief.

Ki sat beside her on the bed and put his arm around her. "How did he know that you and I were—together?"

"I don't know. Someone told him. Men always talk. Anybody who saw us that night. And Korman found out. Ki, I'm afraid of that man. I never wanted to have him in my bed. You must understand that."

"I do, Olivia," said Ki. "I won't let him come near you again."

He could see that she was relieved. "Thank you, Ki," she said. "But perhaps it would be better if I left town. I do not want you to get hurt because of me." She buried her head in his chest and he ran his fingers through her lustrous black hair. "I would kill myself if anything happened to you."

Ki calmed her, then said, "Tell me what you know about the man who was killed the other night. Do you know who did it?"

"Yes," she murmured. "Jorge got drunk and told me. He

91

was boasting about it. Jorge, Señor Korman, and another man did it. That's what he said."

"Did he tell you why they killed the man?"

"No. But I think I know. Señor Adams was a nice young man. He was shy, but he saw what was happening in the valley, and it made him angry to see the Frenchman grabbing all the land and scaring all the ranchers. He told me once that he had been threatened—by Señor Korman and my brother. But he ignored them and kept on doing what he thought was right. I know in my heart that the rich man told Korman and Jorge to hurt Señor Adams. They do not work except by his orders."

Ki was not surprised, but still all he had was Olivia's hearsay of Jorge's boasting "confession." Everyone who knew anything in Augusta surmised that the two killers and the other hired guns at the chateau did nothing except by order from the Marquis—but there was no absolute proof of that. It looked as though Beaumont kept his transactions with Korman off the record; and Korman was skilled enough not to get caught red-handed. A formidable arrangement. Maybe the weak link was Olivia's brother, Jorge.

"Does your brother live up at the chateau?" he asked her.

"Well, not in the house, but in a sleeping shack nearby. Not even Señor Korman lives in the house. I think the lady does not want to share her place with such men. She is from a fine family in New York, I hear. And she is unhappy here. I do not blame her."

Ki looked directly into Olivia's large, sad eyes. "You don't belong here, either," he said. "When this is over, I want you to promise me that you will give up this life and find a home in a decent town. Jessie and I will help you."

"I'd love to live in San Francisco," the girl said dreamily. Then she added in a more somber voice, "But I would like to be where you are, Ki. I—I feel safe when you are around."

He kissed her. Their breath melded hotly. Pulling away,

he said, "Olivia, mine is a warrior's life. I sometimes don't know where I'll be tomorrow or the next day. Most of the time I live with Jessie at the Circle Star, but whenever I must, I travel to many places. And the work I do for her is dangerous. I never know when or if I shall return to the Circle Star. I cannot promise anything, Olivia, not even that I will see you tomorrow."

"I do not want promises," the girl breathed huskily. "I want your love, Ki."

Ki lowered her onto the bed and they lay there in a tight embrace for a long time. Olivia clutched him passionately, gazing into his black eyes. She knew so little about this strange, exciting man—and yet she knew that she loved him as she had loved no other. Her life, up to her meeting with Ki, had been one of rarely interrupted misery—always scraping by, taking humiliating work, sleeping with dirty, uncouth men for a few pesos or a few dollars. Yet all that— all the hard memories—faded from her mind when she felt this man's arms around her. She remembered vividly their lovemaking of two nights ago, and she wanted to recapture that intensity and wild pleasure, that communication with the strong spirit he possessed. Loving Ki made Olivia stronger than she had ever thought possible.

The samurai explored the length of her neck with his mouth, breathing the beautiful scent she carried naturally. This girl was as fragile as a desert flower, and he did not want to hurt her in any way. Gently he lowered her frilly blouse over her shoulders.

She brought Ki's lips to her breasts, holding him there as he sucked and nibbled at her distended brown nipples. A soft sigh escaped Olivia's lips. Her fingers ranged over his tautly muscled back as he sent a white-hot current through her entire body.

Outside her door they could hear the sounds of the saloon below. O'Hare's place was crowded tonight. Ki guessed that one of the patrons had told Korman of the time Ki had spent in Olivia's room; and no doubt some bastard would pass the word of tonight's visit. It was difficult to keep a secret in this town, he imagined. He cursed Korman even as he kissed the girl. He could not get the skinny, narrow-faced man out of his mind. Even more than the scheming Marquis, Niles Korman was a threat to this community—and thereby a threat to the Slash S. Somehow Korman must be neutralized, if not eliminated. As much as Ki hated killing, he would not be sorry to see Korman die.

Olivia said, "What are you thinking, Ki?" She could tell he was lost in a private reverie.

Lifting himself up on one elbow, his free hand softly cupping her exposed breast, Ki told her the truth. "Korman," he said simply.

"Stop it, then," the girl snapped. "I do not want that man in my bed ever again—even in your mind." She reached up to stroke his face. "Think only of me, at least tonight."

She was right, he realized. Nothing could be done about Korman tonight. Jessie would find out what she could from the Marquis. Until he spoke with her about that, Ki was powerless to act. And with this girl in his arms—there was only one thing to do.

Olivia's hand snaked down, traveling over his chest and belly, edging into his pants. He felt himself stiffen at her touch. He rolled over on the bed so that the girl was on top of him. Her breasts hung invitingly above him and he took one in his mouth, toying with it, causing her to gasp. Her hand, though, remained firm in its quest; wrapping her fingers around his hot, pulsing manhood, she held her prize tightly. Slowly, then, she began to massage it, her soft hand slipping along its silky length.

"You are so strong, so big, Ki," she murmured.

"A man is only as strong as the woman he loves," Ki said. His eyes were closed as he experienced the teasing, tingling sensation caused by her fingers.

Working quickly, Ki pulled her dress down to expose her legs and the bushy, fragrant treasure between them. Her blouse remained at her waist. Then, easing himself up, he slid his own pants down to his knees. The urgency they felt was reflected in their faces. Olivia worked her hand to the base of his shaft and down to the pendulous sack that hung below. He gasped involuntarily as her nails scratched him there. Ki held her by her narrow waist and lifted her; the girl planted her strong legs on either side of his and moved at his direction. Ki lowered her over his ramrod. She grasped him and guided him inside. She was tight, but she took him quickly, enveloping every inch of him. Olivia cried out as Ki thrust upward to bury himself in her completely.

Later they lay side by side, gathering their strength. It was long past nightfall now, and the girl's room was shrouded ominously in darkness. Ki sat up and started to put his clothes back on. Olivia, fully naked beneath the quilt, reached for him, not wanting him to go.

"I must leave now," he said. "Jessie will be back later tonight, and she will have spoken to the Marquis. She and Roosevelt are there now."

Olivia Calderon shivered. "I hope she is safe."

"Beaumont would never hurt her directly. It is when she is away from the chateau that I worry."

Ki pulled on his black leather vest and checked its numerous pockets for his hidden weapons. They were all in place. Since he did not like to carry a gun, he made certain that he always carried his slender-bladed *tanto* and a supply of *shuriken* throwing stars. He worked quickly and quietly whenever possible. Gunfire, he found, always drew unwanted attention, and guns were less reliable than his own razor-sharp reflexes.

The girl said, "Ki, I will go away from here if you and Jessie also go away. Why do you stay? It only means danger for you both."

"I thank you for your concern, Olivia," he replied almost

formally. As much as he cared for this girl, he reminded himself not to get too involved—for her sake as well as his own. "But I do not run from a fight; nor does Jessie."

"I didn't mean it like that," Olivia said quietly.

"I know," Ki relented, and sat once again on the bed. He stroked her soft hair. "As much as we hate it, fighting is a part of our lives. Ever since her father died, both of us have vowed to carry on his legacy. It is never easy, and far too often it is dangerous. Therefore I must stay at her side and allow no harm to come to her—or to the memory of Alex Starbuck."

Olivia watched him put his arms through the vest and adjust the *tanto* in its sheath at his waist. He stood and went to the door, and she felt the sting of tears again as he closed the door behind him.

Ki made his way out of the saloon, saluting O'Hare on the way. He knew he was being watched by the other men in the tavern. He, in turn, looked for the men most likely to report to the Marquis or to give him trouble at the rich man's behest. The faces remained strange to him, many of them hostile.

The street was shrouded in darkness, a few weak shafts of light filtering from scattered windows along the way. The September night was chill, and Ki—wearing only a shirt, his leather vest, denim pants, and a pair of rope-soled slippers—felt the cold air against his skin. Yet he was inured to it, through his training and temperament; he was more aware of potential danger than cold. In this town, with the enemies he had already made, he knew he was a highly visible target for the Marquis's men.

Olivia's dilemma troubled him too. On the one hand, if she left Augusta as her brother had ordered, she would be well out of the way if violence broke out; yet he would rather she stayed here, where he could at least try to protect her. Either way, it was a heavy risk—and what angered

96

him most was that it was *her* life on the line, even though she was a threat to no one. Her greatest offense had been in resisting Korman's affections. But who could blame the girl for wanting to keep the loathsome shootist at arm's length?

At this hour, Augusta was eerily quiet, but for the raucous noise from the saloon, which faded as he got farther from it. The narrow, rutted streets were blanketed in shadows that seemed to swallow up the lone man as he walked back to the hotel where he and Jessie were staying. He felt a twinge of anxiety as he thought of her up at the Marquis's house.

Unseen, a figure stepped out from a black alleyway and came up behind Ki. The samurai felt the powerful arms whip around his throat and tighten menacingly, choking off his breath. It never occurred to him to panic, as most men would have done, and thus assure his own death. Instead, he simply relaxed in response to the pressure and thrust his elbows sharply into his attacker's gut. He felt the flesh yield and heard a grunt as his assailant's breath rushed out. The arms loosened; Ki could breathe. He struck again with his elbows, then reached up to grasp the arms around his neck and pry them apart. The man was strong. Ki had no leverage, so he relied on pure strength—and slowly the arms came apart enough for him to drop through and push the man away. Drawing a deep breath, Ki whirled to face his unknown attacker.

In the dense darkness he could make out a large shape and hear the labored breathing of the man. Ki trained his keen eyes on the moving shape, but still could not make out who he was. The odor of hard drink and sweat lingered in the air as the samurai circled slowly, inching closer to the attacker.

The man weaved uncertainly in front of him. He was large but not very tall. Ki heard him mutter a curse and spit at the ground. The oath sounded like Spanish.

"Calderon?" Ki said.

"I kill you, yellow man," Jorge Calderon gritted. "Son of a whore!"

With that, Calderon lunged, moving more quickly than Ki had anticipated. The Mexican's bulk collided with full force against the samurai, knocking Ki to the dirt. With the big man's weight atop him, Ki had to squirm like a serpent beneath a rock to work free. He pushed himself to his feet and assumed his fighting stance. As Calderon struggled to his knees, Ki unleased a savage snap-kick to the Mexican's chin, knocking him back to the ground. Enraged, the Mexican moved more quickly this time, leaping to his feet, cursing.

Now, as his eyes grew more accustomed to the inky darkness of the street, Ki could make out the man's broad, angry face. "Who sent you, Calderon?" he asked, not expecting an answer.

"No one tell Jorge Calderon what to do. I kill you for myself. You defile my sister, son of a whore."

"I did not defile your sister, Calderon. I am her friend. It is Korman who defiled her, if anyone. Can't you see that? Korman is your true enemy—not I." Ki tried to reason with the man, but Calderon heard none of it.

"Your words stink. I will kill you, yellow man."

Ki leaped to his right as Calderon attacked again. The samurai lifted his knee into the Mexican's gut as the big man charged, and doubled him over. That was all Calderon could take. As he turned and straightened, he pulled a knife from his belt. It was a twelve-inch, double-edged fighting knife with a flat blade that shone dully as Calderon waved it in front of him.

In the narrow street, Ki felt constricted, hemmed in. With a knife in his enemy's hands, he knew now that this was a fight to the death. He pondered for a moment whether to try to disarm the crazed Mexican or to draw his own blade and fight steel with steel.

But the choice was taken out of his hands. With a deep-throated growl, Calderon leapt forward, his knife outthrust before him in an attempt to impale Ki. But the samurai sidestepped, sliding his *tanto* in a graceful motion out of its sheath. As the Mexican's momentum carried him forward, Ki reached out with his free hand and pushed his enemy's knife hand aside, then spun around and brought the *tanto* down in a long arc, slicing open the back of Calderon's jacket, but only barely touching flesh.

The sting of the blade brought a howl from Calderon. *"Hijo de puta!* Now I will kill you, *chino!"*

The Mexican attacked again, swinging his blade in an uppercut meant to disembowel Ki, who stepped under the slice and planted a flat-footed kick in the would-be killer's groin.

Calderon grunted and backpedaled swiftly, his eyes registering shock as he waved the twelve-inch blade before him to keep Ki away.

The Mexican, angrier than ever, heaved himself at the samurai. His big knife slicked across Ki's left upper arm, drawing blood. There was little pain, for Ki was concentrating wholly on defeating this man.

Calderon's eyes gleamed with satisfaction. He gained confidence. But Ki defended himself expertly from subsequent thrusts and jabs. Ki shuffled right, then left, his feet stirring up dustclouds as he moved. Calderon stayed on the offensive, driving Ki back. Blood spilled from Ki's arm. With one of Calderon's sweeping thrusts, Ki bent low, avoiding a knife in the neck, and brought himself upright, swinging his own blade across the Mexican's belly. This time it bit into Calderon's paunch and sent him reeling in pain.

*"Madre de Dios!"* he cried.

Ki stepped in again, but Calderon clumsily fended him off. Gripping his wound with his free hand, Calderon muttered under his breath. With each thrusting attack, Ki could feel him losing strength. But Calderon wasn't about to give up. The Mexican, his hand pressing the bloody gut wound, renewed his efforts. He met Ki's blade with his own, steel ringing against steel, and the two stood in a stalemate for several tense, dangerous seconds.

Then Ki reached for Calderon's throat, knowing the man could not defend himself. But the samurai was surprised when Calderon swept his hand away and forgot the bleeding. Ki's own arm was red and wet, but he ignored the injury. Finally the two knives swung free of each other. Ki jabbed again at Calderon's exposed stomach, and missed.

Calderon lunged forward then and desperately held his long knife out to penetrate Ki's heart. He put everything behind the thrust as he barreled forward.

Ki parried the thrust with his own *tanto* and in the same movement plunged the knife into Calderon's stomach, but this time much deeper. He twisted it hard before withdrawing the knife, and pushed the big man away. His face contorted in silent agony, Calderon staggered back, reeling. He ran into a wall and slumped against it, sliding slowly to the ground, blood spilling in a dark puddle from his torn guts.

The samurai bent over him. Calderon, with painful effort, looked up into Ki's face. He attempted a bitter smile, but it was more like a death's-head grin than anything else.

"Yellow man..." he gasped. "My sister...she is in danger...Korman..." His breath came hard and he was losing blood fast.

"Don't try to talk," said Ki. "I will see that your sister is not harmed."

"Korman...kill her if she...if she stays." The words were barely audible. And in the darkness Calderon's face looked as pale as paper.

Ki held the man's head. Life drained from Calderon with the blood that soaked the dirty street. Finally he was dead. Ki let his head fall, and he stood. Why had he been forced to kill this man? Who had sent Jorge after him? Ki could see Korman's prodding behind this. Calderon was not the type of man who acted alone, even to avenge his sister's honor.

Ki looked up, and in the darkness, looming high above the town, he could see the inky silhouette of the Marquis's chateau, lights burning brightly in the many windows. Jessie was up there now, dining with the Frenchman.

As he turned away from the dead Mexican and made his way back to the hotel, he breathed a silent prayer for her safety.

# Chapter 7

The dinner was no less sumptuous, the host no less courtly—but Augusta de Beaumont had excused herself this time, complaining of a headache. The Marquis questioned Jessie and Roosevelt about their trip. "A buffalo is a *magnifique* trophy—very rare these days," he commented, sipping his imported Burgundy wine. "My congratulations, Mr. Roosevelt, for pursuing it as far as you did."

The New Yorker explained that Dennis Hawthorne, the expert guide, was really responsible for tracking and locating the animal. "I had a beautiful opportunity, but I wasn't able to capitalize on it. Next time out, as long as I have Hawthorne with me, I'll bag one."

Jessie was smoldering with impatience. She had wanted to confront Beaumont immediately, but Roosevelt argued for caution and good manners; he wanted to spring the issue on the Frenchman after dinner had begun, to take him off guard as much as possible. She tried to see the logic in this approach, but she was angry with the Marquis, and the more she heard his unctuous voice and witnessed his slippery manners, the more she disliked him. She could not deny the driving intelligence behind those sharp eyes—but there was also ambition and total disregard for human life. And she was growing to hate him for that. She looked across the table. The Frenchman, so impeccably groomed, his dark hair combed back from his high, unlined forehead, met her gaze. He was nothing, she thought to herself, if not bold.

"You have said very little tonight, Miss Starbuck," he offered.

"I have very little to say," she replied.

"But whatever it is, I'll wager it is very important to you."

Jessie glanced at Roosevelt, who was calmly wiping his spectacles with a napkin. She figured that now was as good a time as any, so she plunged ahead.

"I'll tell you what's on my mind, if you're really curious, Marquis. I'm very disturbed about some of the things that are going on here in the valley. In the short time I've been here, I've learned that you're trying to acquire land and cattle from folks who don't want to sell. You've been pretty successful so far, despite strong opposition. Some people have been killed—"

"Not by me," the Marquis said evenly.

"No one has accused you, my good man," Roosevelt said.

"What about Paul Adams, the young newspaper publisher?" Jessie pressed. "Are you saying you didn't want him dead?"

The Marquis sipped his wine calmly, savoring it before answering. He looked directly at his beautiful dinner guest and said, "I cannot say I didn't want that young man out of the way, out of Augusta, and out of the Dakota Territory —but I did not kill him. Perhaps some community-minded citizen took the law into his own hands. Adams was a disruptive character, Miss Starbuck. I was not his only enemy."

"The fact that you were his enemy may have given the others some confidence. If you would profit from Adams's death and the destruction of his newspaper—"

"That is a bold supposition," Beaumont blazed.

"It was a bold murder," Jessie said. She watched the man's face; the Marquis grew redder and his eyes widened in barely controlled vexation. She pushed him further. "And I do not see who would profit as much as you, with the *Chronicle* eliminated. Who else were the paper's enemies?"

Beaumont said, "Miss Starbuck, you have been in the Little Missouri Valley less than four days. How in God's name can you presume to know what goes on behind every closed door here? I simply cannot accept your wild innuendoes as anything more than just that. My aim in this valley is to make it as profitable for as many people as possible. To do so, I am indeed attempting to buy large parcels of land and to purchase cattle to raise on that land. Some shortsighted, stubborn, indeed jealous people refuse to see the merit in my plan and will do anything to oppose me. They only have their own immediate profit in mind; they are not concerned with the good of the entire valley, as I most certainly am."

Jessie instinctively disbelieved him, but she had no way to prove him false. Her green eyes burned. In her gut she knew this man was a skilled liar—and she was beginning to feel that he was even more dangerous because of the very ease with which he mouthed his lies. And what gave him such overweening confidence? How much money did he really have? And further, was it all his own money—or did the Marquis have secret backers?

The final question brought Jessie back to one of her original suspicions—that the Marquis de Beaumont might somehow be tied in to the European-based business cartel that had killed her father. Perhaps it was a bit farfetched to assume that Beaumont, because of his European background, was linked to the hated syndicate. But, she reminded herself, there was his wife, Augusta Heufer, whose father was an internationally prominent financier. Or was that just more wishful thinking on her part?

Roosevelt was saying, "I don't think Jessie is actually accusing you, Marquis. She is very concerned, however, since she too is a landowner in this valley. I myself have developed an interest in acquiring a ranch hereabouts. But if conditions remain uncertain—that is, if the violence continues—I would think twice about investing here." The New Yorker was trying a different form of leverage.

The Marquis regained his composure. Jessie's attacks had taken him off guard, as had been her design. He refilled his guests' wineglasses. "That is a good point, Mr. Roosevelt," he acknowledged. "When I founded Augusta, I was perhaps too—what shall I say?—idealistic. I had hoped that traditional law agencies would not be necessary in a decent community peopled by honest, hardworking men and women. I see now that I may have been mistaken."

"Then you would not object if the territorial law was called in to investigate Paul Adams's murder?" Jessie prodded.

Addressing himself to Roosevelt, Beaumont continued, "I can see now that there is a need for a local marshal in Augusta. I shall consider appointing one immediately, with the approval of the town council, of course."

"Of course," Jessie echoed. For the Marquis even to consider such a step was an improvement. Was he feeling that his back was to the wall?

Roosevelt asked Beaumont about the town council. From the Frenchman's description, however, it was clear that the council was far from independent—more like a rubber stamp for the Marquis's policies.

Jessie pressed for a more specific commitment. "If you appoint a marshal, will he be accountable to you? Or to the townspeople? Why not hold an election instead?"

The Marquis smiled thinly. "Oh, do not mistake my intentions, Miss Starbuck. I am a committed democrat. In my country there is a long tradition of rebellion against the authority of kings. Even if my own family has often been on the opposite side, I remain in favor of rights for the common man. I am a great admirer of the philosopher Rousseau—and of your Thomas Jefferson. Great men with great ideas. Unfortunately, as I said previously, idealism often does not bring the desired results. I shall first appoint a constabulary, with the council's approval, and then we shall establish the electoral mechanism of which you Americans are so fond."

"I daresay the process works pretty successfully," Roosevelt interjected. "I've seen my share of corruption in Albany, but most of my fellow assemblymen are dedicated public servants."

Jessie, whose opinion of politicians was generally a low one, said, "It's still a better system than one-man rule. I'm surprised the people of the town have stood for it for so long."

"They have not been hurt, nor have the ranchers in the valley, by my strong but benevolent 'rule,' if you will."

"I just don't buy it, Marquis," Jessie persisted. "Paul Adams was hurt. One of the most respected cattlemen in the valley was hurt. People who don't sell out to you have been hurt—unable to get help at roundup time, perhaps, like my own man at the Slash S. I'm making Clark King my partner in the ranch, you know—half-owner."

"Congratulations to King," the Frenchman said without enthusiasm. "I assure you I have nothing to do with any man's choice of working or not working in the valley."

"Then who does—Niles Korman and the boys?"

"Mr. Korman works for me in a limited capacity—to ensure the security of my person and my property. What he does on his own time is of no concern to me—though I doubt you could prove he has been involved in wrongdoing, Miss Starbuck."

Roosevelt watched the sparks fly between Beaumont and Jessie. The servants moved into the dining room to clean off the table. Again the Marquis refilled the wineglasses. Amid the muted clatter of dishes, Jessie glared across the table at her host. When she thought of Paul Adams, of Ki's encounter with Korman and Calderon, of what Clark King had told her about the Frenchman's strongarm tactics, she wondered how the hell she could pin this man down. Damn, he was slippery!

They adjourned to the Marquis's library. Jessie looked around at this male domain, the dark paneled walls lined with leatherbound books and portraits of Beaumont's distinguished ancestors. A fire crackled in a big marble-encased fireplace, and the Marquis invited them to sit in the big leather chairs arranged in a semicircle near the bright, noisy flame. Jessie and Roosevelt faced the Frenchman, who ordered brandy from the silent, straight-backed butler. When the butler returned with the glasses, Jessie took hers moodily. This evening was not going as she had anticipated.

The Marquis broke the silence, saying, "Miss Starbuck, I wish there were some way to convince you that my intentions are not wholly self-serving. I do admit that I believe my plans for this valley will enrich me beyond all my former imaginings. And I do intend to become very rich, Miss Starbuck. The Badlands, as you Americans call this territory, are a rich and beautiful country, ready to be exploited. My refrigerated railroad cars, running along the important northern overland route, will make cattle ranching increasingly profitable in the coming years. The smaller ranchers cannot grasp that—which is why I am trying to buy them out now, before their stubbornness causes them *and* me to lose money. Surely you can see that."

"I can see how your tactics have made people afraid of you. I can see how you have disrupted lives and—perhaps indirectly, perhaps not—caused others to die. I do not consider myself shortsighted, Marquis. I am a businesswoman with a large company and many scattered interests to maintain. But I abhor violence as a business tactic."

"You are a wealthy young woman," the Marquis went on, deflecting her repeated challenge. "Don't you desire to increase your father's legacy? Surely he would wish you to increase the profits of his far-ranging business empire."

Jessie muttered her acknowledgment, wondering what he was driving at.

The Marquis turned to Roosevelt. "And you, sir, have expressed an interest in investing in the Little Missouri Valley. A marvelous idea indeed. There is an abundance of suitable ranchland stretching up the river more than a hundred miles. One could almost choose a site blindfolded and retire on the returns from two or three years of business."

"I like what I've seen so far," Roosevelt said. "But I have no intention of retiring quite yet."

Beaumont gave a short laugh. "A man after my own heart. It occurs to me that instead of arguing means, we should agree upon a common end, one that will benefit us equally."

"Get to the point, Marquis," Jessie said with unconcealed impatience. She was exasperated, at the end of her tether with this man.

Roosevelt leaned forward, balancing his brandy glass on his knee. He, too, was interested to learn what the Frenchman had up his finely tailored sleeve.

"Pardon my circumlocutions. It is a trait we Frenchmen share, no matter how long we live in another country. We love to talk." He gestured absently with his pale, long-fingered hand. "We also love money and the immense satisfaction it brings: fine objects, comfort in old age, something to leave our children. I confess that I possess these fancies, that I am a typical Frenchman and proud of it. However, another characteristic of the French is generosity.

109

We do not desire to hoard our good fortune. Rather, we see the virtue in sharing with friends. And if I am not stretching the meaning of that word—*friend*—I should like to share with you two my good fortune."

"The Slash S is doing fine for me," Jessie said in a not-too-friendly tone.

"I'm certain it is. But what do you think about the possibility of sharing as a full partner in control of the entire valley?" Beaumont's eyes glowed now, and it wasn't from the fire. It was an inner light that possessed him and glinted out at Jessie. His gaunt, handsome features were clouded now in a misty, almost sinister ambition.

"I want you to consider this, Miss Starbuck: a one-third share in a vast cattle and shipping enterprise that will one day encompass not only this valley"—he waved his hand in a gesture of insignificance—"but the entire Dakota Territory. One day it will be a state, my father-in-law assures me. He has friends in Washington; he knows these things. And when that happens, we will own virtually everything. Imagine that!"

He turned then to Roosevelt. The Easterner was drinking in everything and growing suspicious of the Frenchman's sudden switch from defending his actions to this outrageous proposal. "And you, sir," the Marquis said, "are to be the third partner. Your family is one of the most prestigious in New York. Mr. Heufer is very well acquainted with them and could have no objections to your joining us in this venture. You have seen the beauty of this country—and its potential. What do you say?"

Roosevelt said simply, "Why? Why would you want us as partners?"

Jessie added, "I suppose you'd rather have us on your side than fighting you—is that it?"

Laughing, the Marquis paused to taste his brandy, then said, "You are an exceptionally intelligent young lady, Miss

Starbuck. Well-bred and capable of appreciating subtleties that escape others of a less discriminating nature. Of course I do not want to fight you." He lowered his glass. "I would fight, if that were the only way," he said quietly. "But that would be to our mutual disadvantage. Surely you can see that."

"You want to monopolize the entire territory," she said, breathless at the audacity of the man. "You'll have to fight a lot of people, Marquis, not just me."

"Really, my good man," the New Yorker put in, "you cannot expect us to endorse such a scheme. Why, it's— it's not the American way. It's against everything we believe in. Business empires and monopolies are the exception, not the rule here. What you propose is an oligarchy—nothing that approaches democracy."

The Marquis chuckled again. He offered Roosevelt a cigar from a large wooden humidor. Roosevelt declined, but the Frenchman took one for himself, pierced the end, lighted it with an elaborate, silver-encased tinderbox, and said, "Oh, no, I've already told you, Mr. Roosevelt, that I am a committed democrat. But in order to provide the stability such a system requires, one must not allow loose ends, as you Americans say. One must provide the people with common purpose, a common will. Only then shall they come together to work to meet their own needs."

"I believe the people themselves provide that common purpose, Marquis," Roosevelt argued. "It works from the bottom up, not from the top down."

Tilting his head curiously, Beaumont said, "A curious remark from a Republican, sir."

"I am not oppposed to business per se," Roosevelt corrected him, "but I am opposed to business *domination* of any city town, or state in the Union."

Jessie could hold back no longer. "And what about the lives of the people who don't see things your way, Marquis?" she asked point-blank. "What's to become of them?"

"Healthy disagreements are inevitable," the Marquis allowed. "Though, if there is a threat to the general welfare—"

"It'll be met in the same way the *Chronicle*'s 'threat' was," she said.

Bolting to his feet, the Frenchman knocked over his brandy glass. He ignored the crash as it splintered on the table and the contents dripped onto the carpeted floor. His face was flushed with anger. "I have made a proper business proposition, Miss Starbuck, but you insist there is something improper about it—and about all my activities. Until you can prove your outrageous theories, I must ask you to desist," he blazed.

"Improper!" Jessie raised her eyebrows as if in surprise. "I'm not suggesting impropriety. I'm accusing you of murder, Marquis."

"Jessie—" Roosevelt cautioned, a hand on her arm.

"Miss Starbuck requires more than a restraining hand," Beaumont declared, looking down at her. "She requires a complete education in the ways of the world. She must learn she cannot insult those who could do her the most good; she must learn not to offend those who are in a position to hurt her."

"Is that a threat?" Jessie demanded, coming to her feet. She faced the Frenchman eye to eye.

Roosevelt stood beside her, ready to prevent her from physical action. He had never seen a woman as angry as this beautiful Texan. And he didn't want her to get hurt.

"I do not make threats, Miss Starbuck," Beaumont replied smoothly. "I simply act as I see fit." He looked her up and down with contempt. "Perhaps my wife was right about you after all." He turned his back on his two visitors, his signal that they were dismissed.

Outside, Jessie did not speak until she and Roosevelt were in the wagon on the way back to Augusta. The town slept darkly below them, and the only sound was the clopping of the horses' hooves and the creaking of the wagon wheels. When they were well away from the chateau she finally said, "Teddy, I could not hold myself in. Beneath that polished French manner, that man is as deadly as a rattlesnake. I've seen the type before, believe me."

"His good manners collapsed fairly quickly, once you laid into him," the New Yorker said with plain admiration in his voice. "You are pretty deadly yourself, my dear Miss Starbuck."

For the first time in what seemed like days, Jessie laughed. "I was afraid for a while that you believed him, Teddy. You certainly didn't lose your temper, thank God."

"I was too amazed at you. Jessie, I know you believe you're in the right, but I think you shouldn't have challenged him openly like that. He is not to be trusted—and we are no longer welcome in his house."

"We got what we came for. And I don't want to go back in his cold, empty house. I wonder what his wife said about me? I could say a few choice things about her."

It was Roosevelt's turn to laugh, baring his large teeth, his entire frame shaking with mirth. "I imagine you'd have no trouble at all," he said.

The sound of the slap echoed off the walls of Olivia's small room. She whimpered, trying desperately not to cry out, to keep it inside herself. She did not want to give the bastard the satisfaction.

Korman looked down at Olivia, on her knees, a thread of blood escaping her nose. He had put his strong hands to good use tonight. By her actions, she had asked to be punished, and he had given it to her good. With the back of his hand he came around again and caught her left cheek, ripping his hand across it and away. He held her head up by the hair.

"Bitch," he muttered between his teeth.

"Please," she whispered, "leave me alone, Señor. I have done nothing—"

Ki had been gone just a few minutes when Korman burst into the room. The skinny man had moved as quickly as a mountain cat, snatching her out of bed, naked, and forcing her to her knees. The only thing for which she could be grateful was that Korman had not forced her to perform a disgusting sex act with him.

"Don't hurt me anymore," she pleaded, bring her hands to her face to touch the bruises there.

"Take your hands off your face. I won't hurt you— much. But I told you to stay away from that yellow-skinned bastard. I told you to get the hell out of town. Your brother told you, too. You don't hear so good, Olivia."

"I—I'll go, Señor. I promise I'll go."

"Why should I believe you? How can I be sure you won't run to your yellow man?" He opened his mouth like a fish and gave out a gurgling laugh, his thin face stretched by the unusual effort. "I know because your Jap-man lover is going to take a knife in the back tonight and he won't be there to run to."

"No—don't hurt him!" Olivia looked up at her tormentor's ugly slash of a face. "I'll kill you if you hurt him!"

"Ha, girlie, the hell you will. You won't live till next Sunday if you cross me. You better make your pretty ass scarce around this town."

She knew him well enough to believe him. She hated this strange, cruel man who had come into her life and her brother's and changed them both for the worse. But she vowed not to let him endanger Ki—even if she had to pay with her own worthless life to stop him.

Niles Korman released the girl, letting the thick black hair fall from his smooth, strong hands. He liked what he saw—Olivia bloodied and beaten, cowering at his feet. He didn't give a damn about her threat. What could she do, after all, a mere woman?

"If I see you again," he sneered, "it'll go much worse for you." Korman stepped away from her, toward the door. "I've gotta find your no-good brother. I hope he did what he was told—or else I wouldn't give a rat's ass for his life, neither." With that the gunman slammed the door, leaving the girl alone with her grief and pain.

His own busted nose still hurt, and he touched it gingerly. He stalked down the narrow staircase and through the Dog's Eye Saloon, pushing men out of his way needlessly. The scowl on his scarred mouth told them to stand back and let him push. Outside, Korman looked into the darkness, up and down the street. He remembered where he was to meet the Mex, and went there. No Mex.

After a year in Augusta, Korman knew every street and alley of the town. And he hated every inch of the place. To him, it stunk of smallness and defeat. Korman thought of himself as cut out for better things than working for the crazy-mad, rich Frenchie, though he enjoyed his work much of the time. His work? Making fear live in the hearts and minds of little men, bending them to the Marquis's will, doing hard and dirty things in the nighttime, dealing death when there was no other way.

Korman had started out in Chicago, where he was born. He had worked for a while, as a skinny but able kid, in one of the great slaughterhouses, where he learned the smell of blood. He didn't mind that smell so much; it was the job he hated, a dull, difficult job, hauling guts and other unusable parts to the incinerator. He hated the place where he lived, and hated his family—an old mother and a sister. His old man had died, drunk, his head split open under a wagon wheel, when Korman was only ten. By the time he was sixteen, the kid had had enough and set out for parts unknown, telling nobody; he just had to get out.

In the years that followed he drifted, honing his skills with cards and weapons, eventually reaching California, where he had his first serious brush with the law. He was broke and hoped to make some cash playing cards. He wanted money badly enough to cheat—and he got caught. He had to shoot a man to stay alive himself, and then he had to run. A posse caught up with him in the mountains a few days later. Korman gave up without a fight, knowing they'd have killed him if he'd given them a chance. A trial of sorts followed, and he was found not guilty for lack of evidence; no one testified against him. After that he left California and never returned.

Korman hired himself out to anybody who would pay—bankers, ranchers, teamsters, anybody who needed protection and could afford him. He stayed mostly on the right side of the law wherever he worked, and earned a good reputation in the cattlemen's clubs and banking association boardrooms. There was never a shortage of work. When the Marquis came along, Korman could name his price—and did. He was earning a hefty wage for this piece of work in Augusta. The toughest part of the job was keeping track of numbskulls like Jorge Calderon. He hoped the Mex had done his job and eliminated the troublesome Japanese who had humiliated Korman the other night. His damned nose ached. . . .

But there was no sign of Calderon, or Ki. Had Korman miscalculated? He had figured that with Jessie Starbuck dining with the boss, the Jap would stay in town and stick his nose into everybody's business but his own. Then, as Korman turned onto a darkened back street, he saw a pair of legs extending from an alley. He went to the body, only to discover Jorge Calderon.

"Goddamned lame-brain Mex," he muttered.

He examined the body and found the deep, clean knife wound that had killed the man. He pocketed the few dollars Calderon had on him, and pulled the body farther into the shelter of the alley. He'd arrange for the disposal of the corpse tonight, before the sun rose and the townspeople got a whiff of this latest fiasco.

*Damn,* he cursed inwardly, *I should never have trusted him with this job. I'll have to deal with the Jap-man myself.*

He returned to the chateau. It was past midnight by the time he got there. He dispatched two men to see after the Mexican's body, then attended to the more unpleasant part of his duties—calling on his boss, the Frenchman.

Luckily the Marquis had not retired. He was in the library, brooding over his brandy. "What do you want, Korman?" he asked shortly, without looking up.

Korman helped himself to a drink before replying. He wanted to remind the Marquis that theirs was a professional relationship—subject to the niceties and manners demanded by mutual respect. Occasionally Beaumont forgot Korman's status, and Korman had to remind him—subtly, of course—that accepting the Marquis's paycheck did not make him an inferior.

"I thought you'd want to know. Jorge Calderon is dead. The Japanese man, Ki, killed him." Korman stated the facts bluntly, taking the chair opposite the Marquis.

"Miss Starbuck's companion is a resourceful man," Beaumont said, a pencil-thin eyebrow raised above his left eye. "You should not have sent the Mexican after him. You should have gone yourself."

"I will, next time," the gunman said thinly. He was speaking to himself as much as to the Marquis, knowing that it had been the only way, all along.

The Frenchman puffed languidly on his cigar, smoke wreathing his head as he pondered something. Korman waited; he knew how the Marquis worked. The silence between them was electric. Several long minutes later the Marquis spoke.

"I dined tonight with Miss Starbuck and Mr. Roosevelt. Two very stubborn persons. I realize now that I underestimated them. I offered them equal shares in my company—knowing they would not accept. They are too idealistic. They will never succeed out here in the American West,

117

for they are not ruthless enough. And yet they are tough, especially Miss Starbuck. Apparently so is her bodyguard, this Ki. Be that as it may, I wish to bend her to my purposes. I do not wish to hurt her, but to hurt something close to her."

"What about that Roosevelt fellow? Easy enough to wing him, to do some damage to his knee or something," Korman suggested.

"No, he must not be touched. His family is acquainted with mine. No—" An idea dawned on Beaumont. "It will be easy enough to get him out of the way, and soon." He scribbled something on a nearby piece of paper.

"But we must get to Miss Starbuck, quickly and effectively—without allowing her to fight back." He drummed the table with his manicured fingertips. Smoke drifted from his lips. "My superiors would never forgive me if I did not capitalize on this chance to destroy the Starbuck empire."

The fingers ceased their drumming. Korman remained alert. He had come to have a grudging admiration for this strange man with the foreign ways and sometimes outlandish costumes and delicate demeanor. Beneath the flamboyant dandy, though, was a mind as hard as steel, as sharp as a bowie knife.

"What is the riding time to the Slash S ranch and back?" the Frenchman asked.

"I'd calculate it at just under four hours, on fresh horses."

The Marquis smiled vaguely, puffing on his cigar. He seemed to enjoy the taste of this particular brand of tobacco. He went on, "Take three men and ride to the Slash S. You should arrive just before dawn. Rest the horses a bit for the ride back." The Marquis weighed his next words very carefully. "Don't kill the woman," he said simply.

"I could do that myself," Korman said. "I don't need three men."

"Do as I say. I do not want to take chances. You said

118

the Mexican could handle Ki by himself. You were wrong."

"Hell, that Mex—"

"Do not question my orders!" the Marquis snapped bluntly.

Korman shot to his feet. "Look, mister," the gunslinger said with a dangerous edge of annoyance, "I'll take your orders for just as long as I want to and as long as I get paid decent. But don't think you own me—because nobody owns Niles Korman. Got it?"

"Oh, I've 'got it,' all right, Mr. Korman. Sit down, won't you? I apologize for my short temper this evening. I am merely ensuring your safety. I wish to keep you well and fit for a long time to come. And when Miss Starbuck decides she wants to fight, I want you to be here to fight her."

"That's what I do best," Korman replied, sitting down again in the soft chair near the fire.

"Once the Kings are eliminated, Miss Starbuck will be what you Americans call 'hopping mad.' I anticipate that she will react quickly and directly. She will have the help of her friend Ki and, I'm certain, Mr. Hawthorne."

"What about Roosevelt?" Korman asked.

"He will be out of town by tomorrow evening," Beaumont said confidently.

Korman didn't bother to ask how. He knew the Marquis had already come up with a plan. He said, "With Calderon gone, I'm short a man."

"How many men do you have, then?"

"Six, besides me," said Korman.

"That should suffice. And if need be, I can arm myself. I am an excellent shot, you know."

Korman did know; he had seen the Marquis practicing with his various expensive rifles and shotguns. But Korman had never seen him fire a gun to kill a man.

As if anticipating Korman's question, Beaumont said, "Do not worry, Monsieur, I have killed men in my life. I shall not hesitate if it comes to that." Now he was puffing jauntily on the cigar and blowing smoke rings in the air. "In my native France I fought two duels and won them both. Honor and fortune must be defended with the force of arms—that is a truth I recognize above all others. You needn't fear that I shall fall short in the heat of battle."

Korman grunted in acknowledgment. Time would tell; it was inevitable that when Jessica Starbuck learned about the Slash S foreman, she would attack the Marquis.

"I want you back here by ten o'clock at the latest," the Frenchman told Korman. "There will be work to do at the chateau. I shall see that Augusta is on the ten o'clock stagecoach to Denver. She has been wanting to get away from here, to do some shopping. This will be her chance." He smiled in a self-satisfied way at the thought of surprising his wife with this unexpected news.

"You expect them to ride against the house?" Korman asked. "They're not that crazy. They must know I have six men. And I can count on as many or more in town in a pinch."

"No, they are not crazy, as you put it. They are extremely intelligent. Miss Starbuck would never ride into your guns without an equal number on her side. That is why we must fortify the chateau. *We* do not want to be taken by surprise. Jessica Starbuck is a resourceful young woman, if the reports I hear are true."

Puzzled, but relieved to see that the Marquis was acting cautiously rather than overconfidently, Korman got up to leave. "Anything else?" he asked.

"Yes," Beaumont replied. "When you get back, send one of the men to me. I shall have an important telegraph message to send."

"Sure," said Korman. He left the Marquis with his brandy and his fire.

The Marquis busied himself composing the telegraph

message. It was perhaps the most important one he had ever sent. Addressing it to his father-in-law, W. H. Heufer, in care of the International Merchants' Bank of New York, Beaumont requested that a message be sent to Theodore Roosevelt, asking him to return home, saying that his wife was ill. That would get the meddlesome Easterner out of Augusta, no questions asked.

Then the Marquis added an optimistic postscript to the telegraph:

FORESEE RESOLUTION TO STARBUCK PROBLEM IMME-DIATELY. INFORM EUROPEAN ASSOCIATES ACCORD-INGLY. WILL WIRE UPON TERMINATION OF BUSINESS AT HAND. YOURS BEAUMONT.

As he watched the fire die, he finished his brandy and calculated the acreage he would gain from the acquisition of the Slash S spread.

★

# Chapter 8

Jessie and Ki pushed their mounts hard. The sun was already
well up in the crystalline sky, warming the earth and dis-
pelling the coldness of the night. But there was an unspoken
urgency in the clear air as they put the miles behind them.
In contrast to their previous ride with Hawthorne and Roosevelt, this time the Badlands landscape appeared bleak and
forbidding, the black buttes and twisted, stunted trees echoing the sense of stark unreality that the two riders somehow
shared.

When they stopped to water their horses, Jessie finally
said, "What's wrong, Ki? In my bones I feel something is
terribly wrong. After I came back last night from seeing the
Marquis—and you told me about Calderon—I felt weak
and sad. Something has happened, but I don't know what
it is."

Ki swallowed a mouthful of water from his canteen and
passed it to her. "I, too, feel this strangeness. This Marquis
is an evil man, Jessie, no matter how smooth and polite he
seems. He is capable of anything. I ask myself if he was
behind Calderon's attack on me. I do not know, but I will
not be surprised by anything that happens now. Olivia sus-
pects that her brother and Korman were responsible for the

death of Paul Adams—at Beaumont's orders. He is dangerous, Jessie. He is a killer."

"I just don't know, Ki. I mean, I know you are right, but we don't have any hard evidence yet. He acted as baffled by the Adams killing as anybody else—but there is a cold ruthlessness beneath his civilized surface. I have never met anyone who operates quite like him. And—" She broke off, her thoughts racing wildly, trying to piece the mystery together.

"What are you thinking, Jessie?" Ki asked after they had remounted.

"Well, it's something that occurred to me last night, Ki. The Marquis has lots of money—we know that. And he is well connected in Europe, and in New York, through his wife's family, the Heufers. They are a banking family—very influential. I just wonder . . . he seems to know an awful lot about me and to be very interested in the Slash S property. I wonder if the cartel isn't sponsoring him. He's a perfect front for their interests in the Dakota Territory. And if he gains control of this valley—"

"He'll be the most powerful man in the territory. And any Starbuck challenge will be met with strong opposition," Ki concluded.

"Perhaps it was just a ploy for him to try to get me to join up with him. That would make it easier for him to acquire more land more quickly. He's awfully smart—maybe too smart—and ambitious."

Ki looked over at Jessie, the woman whose life and fortune he had dedicated his own life to protecting. Beautiful, yes—he never tired of gazing at her pleasing, clean features and flaming hair, as well as her slender, well-shaped figure. She was as intelligent and quick as any man she came up against—even smarter than most. He would be damned if this Marquis harmed her or endangered her legacy. And if it was true that the hated cartel had something to do with the Frenchman's dealings in the Little Missouri Valley, then the Marquis de Beaumont was doubly cursed and would die doubly hard. Ki would see to that.

"Dennis does not trust him, never has," Jessie went on. "Teddy is beginning to see the truth, though he's still sort of ambivalent." She laughed at that. "His word, 'ambivalent.' He says that's what comes of being in politics. One cannot afford to make up one's mind very quickly because there's always another side to the issue."

"Surely Roosevelt can see what the Marquis is doing."

Jessie said, "Yes, but he hates to think anyone—especially a man as privileged and wealthy as the Marquis—is capable of dirty dealing. He likes to look on the bright side of things, Teddy does. But he'll have to face reality on this matter, sooner or later. He's talking about buying some land in the valley to build a ranch for himself. The Marquis doesn't like the idea one bit."

"Hawthorne is the one who knows the Frenchman best. I would trust his opinion over Roosevelt's," Ki said.

Jessie, when thinking of Dennis Hawthorne, could not help thinking of their time together two nights ago. She longed for him, to be close to him in this hour of danger. She wondered where he had gone today. When she had checked his room, she was told he had ridden out before dawn this morning. She hoped he would be careful, because she still feared that something was amiss out here.

The two riders were on Starbuck land before noon, with a long way to go before they reached the ranch house. Jessie wanted to meet with Clark and Georgie King to discuss their strategy in facing the Marquis's threatening presence in the valley. Jessie had no intention of giving up the Slash S spread or of abandoning the Kings. In her first encounter with the foreman and his vivacious, pregnant wife, she had been impressed by their strong commitment to the land and to the Starbuck interests. They had done a good job of nurturing the herd and keeping the ranch operating efficiently. The main problem now was fall roundup. Clark King had said it would be difficult to hire men to work the roundup, thanks to the Frenchman's stranglehold on labor in the valley. If necessary, Jessie thought, she and Ki and Hawthorne—and maybe even Roosevelt—would work the roundup. The seed herd was still small enough that it wouldn't take many hands to do the job properly.

Jessie worried, though, about the woman, Georgie—so close to giving birth. Jessie would see that she got the best care when the time came. The Kings were risking enough in living on the Slash S; Jessie couldn't ask them to risk their first child. . . .

Ki signaled ahead. The ranch house was in sight, a thin ribbon of smoke rising from the chimney into the cloudless sky. Jessie rode up beside her companion. She saw the troubled look on his angular face. "What is it, Ki?"

The samurai shook his head. "I don't know, Jessie. There's danger here. Perhaps you should stay back and let me approach the house. I'll call for you when I know it's safe."

"Don't be ridiculous, Ki. If there's anything wrong, I want to be with you." She reached for his arm, gripping it tightly. "I hope there isn't anything—"

"We'll find out soon enough," Ki said. "I may be wrong."

He wasn't. As they approached the small house and the outbuildings, both of them knew something was horribly amiss here. There was no sign of the Kings, except the smoke from the chimney. An ominous silence hung over the yard outside the house. Then they saw that the door was open.

Jessie and Ki glanced at each other and dismounted, then walked into the house.

"Oh, my God!" Jessie cried, bringing her hands to her face.

There, on the kitchen floor, was the mangled, bloody

body of young Randolph King. There were at least a dozen bullet wounds from which blood had flowed to form a wide stain on the crude wooden floor. Jessie bent over him as Ki went back outside. The boy's hair covered his face. The old brass-mounted Enfield rifle lay broken beside him.

A terrifying, animal-like scream brought Jessie bolt upright. She whirled, her .38 Colt filling her fist in a smooth, easy motion. The gun was cocked and aimed—at Georgie King. The woman sat huddled in a far corner of the house, screaming like a banshee. Jessie went to her.

Ki returned to the house and saw the source of the unearthy howl. "Mr. King is around back, Jessie—dead," he told her.

The woman howled again, even louder. Jessie knelt beside her, but Georgie King did not even see her. The woman's eyes were glazed, her face streaked, her hair wildly disheveled. Her dress was torn and she held it to her breast with a shaking hand. The eyes remained unfocused even as Jessie attempted to get the woman's attention.

"Georgie," she said softly.

"Oh, holy God, they killed him! They killed my husband!" Mrs. King shrieked. Her mouth moved as if by its own accord. The words came from somewhere deep inside her. She was in deep shock, heaving for breath. Her gravid belly moved up and down, and sweat dripped from her face.

"Georgie," Jessie said urgently, "tell me who did this. Who killed your husband and nephew? Can you tell me? I'm here to help you." She almost choked on the words as she looked at the woman's terror-stricken face.

"They killed him!" Georgie King screamed. "Dear Jesus! He's dead!"

"Who, Georgie?" But it was no good and Jessie knew it. The woman was too far gone.

Ki took the boy's body outside as Jessie attempted to make the woman comfortable. She covered Georgie with a blanket and laid her down on the floor. Still, Georgie King cried out in pain and terror, "Leave us alone! Go away, don't hurt us! We never—!" Then she arched her back and screamed, a bloodcurdling outburst.

Jessie didn't know much about birthing babies, but she knew enough to realize that Georgie was in shock-induced labor. The woman winced and brought her hands to her belly. Ki reappeared and asked what was happening.

"She's having the baby," Jessie said. "I'm not sure what to do."

The samurai put some water on the stove to boil as Jessie tried to ease the woman's pain. Georgie squeezed Jessie's proffered hand, her eyes closed, her mind fled. Jessie wanted to cry, but there wasn't time.

Ki said, "Stay with her, Jessie. I'll bury the men. Call for me when it is time. It could be several hours." He looked down upon the stricken woman. "She didn't deserve this."

"I know," agreed Jessie. "Neither did Clark or the boy. And somebody's going to pay for this," she added gravely.

She sat with Georgie King for two hours as the woman's agony continued. Every few minutes the woman would cry out for her husband, and Jessie tried to soothe her—but it was useless. The labor pains grew more frequent, and Jessie found several clean towels and poured the steaming water into a porcelain pitcher. Washing her own hands, she cursed her bad timing and bad judgment. If only she had anticipated this attack or stayed to help the Kings defend themselves— if only she had seen how serious the battle for the rich Little Misery land had become!

Returning to the suffering woman, Jessie eased down beside her. Georgie clutched her hand now, moaning and tossing her head. The woman's breath became more ragged and her breast heaved. Then she cried out loudly, "Oh, oh, dear Lord, it's coming! God, God—!"

Jessie called for Ki, who came running. Outside, the sun was well into its long slide down in the west. He had just finished his grim task in time to help Jessie.

A tense, painful half hour later, they safely delivered Georgie King of a red-faced, bawling baby boy. Jessie tenderly cleaned him and severed the umbilical cord that bound him to his stricken mother. The boy was very small but seemed healthy, and Jessie was relieved. As she held the naked, wailing infant she felt a strange wholeness, despite her grief for the King family; it was as if the cycle of life had been completed, for even in the midst of death, here was new life just beginning. And she wondered what would become of this helpless child and his mother.

The woman, her face pale and wet, lay still, her mind resting from the relentless shock of the previous several hours. Ki tended to her, bathing her face and trying to comfort her. But slowly the life drained out of her as she gave up the fight. She had stayed alive to give the baby a chance—but now she was going to join her husband, to whom she called out now and then.

"Clark...Clark..." she murmured, half-conscious.

When Jessie tried to show her the baby, Georgie did not respond. The pain of loss was too much for her. The baby was of this world and the mother already of the next.

Jessie wept for her, a mother who would never know her own child. Georgie King died late in the afternoon, and Ki took the body outside for burial with the others. Jessie, worried about the baby, bundled it in a clean basket and prepared the Kings' wagon. She set out for Augusta as Ki dug the woman's grave. He would catch up with Jessie when he could, bringing their horses. On the lonely ride back to town, Jessie Starbuck shed no more tears. She vowed, simply, to avenge these deaths, no matter who were the murderers or what price she herself had to pay.

Dennis Hawthorne listened intently to Jessie's story. Roosevelt fiddled with his glasses, but he, too, was taking in every word. They were gathered in the Easterner's room.

129

Ki stood apart, in the shadows, silently observing the others.

He had joined Jessie a mile outside of Augusta, and the two of them had ridden in the rest of the way together. Ki had seen to the horses as Jessie located a local midwife and left the baby there in the woman's care, promising to return for the child in a day or two. Then she had called on Roosevelt and Hawthorne.

When she finished talking, Roosevelt said, "Such savagery! By the Almighty, I do not understand my fellow man!"

Hawthorne stonily ignored the Easterner. He spoke to Jessie and Ki. "I was out at the Slash S this morning, too," he said.

Jessie fixed her gaze on him. "What do you mean, Dennis?"

"I didn't get to the house, but I came within a couple miles of it when I saw them." He paused. Jessie, Ki, and Roosevelt were rigid with curiosity. "There were four riders, but I only recognized one for sure—Niles Korman. They were circling west before heading back to town. I stayed out of sight and followed them. I figured they were looking for stray Slash S beef or cutting fences or something. They took their time getting back to Augusta. They got in about nine and headed direct to Beaumont's house. That's when I came looking for you, Jessie. I heard you had gone out to the ranch and I figured that since Korman and his boys were here in Augusta, you wouldn't be seeing them today. I didn't have any idea they'd been to the house. If I'd known—"

"You couldn't have known, Dennis," Jessie said. She glanced at Ki. "None of us expected this."

"The Marquis?" Roosevelt whispered. "Is he responsible for this massacre?"

"Looks that way," said Hawthorne. "I need a drink. You got anything to drink, Roosevelt?"

The Easterner gestured toward a nearby cabinet, and Hawthorne went to pour himself a drink. He swallowed one shot quickly and poured another. Then he went back to his chair and sipped the whiskey. Jessie paced the floor, her eyes darting from Ki to Roosevelt to Hawthorne. Roosevelt fixed his spectacles back on his nose. No one spoke for several long minutes.

Then Hawthorne said, "I'll be happy to shoot the bastard myself. And his bitch of a wife if necessary. And Korman. And any of his boys."

"More killing," Jessie said evenly. The idea was repugnant to her, yet she knew it would probably become necessary. After what she had seen at the Kings, after Ki's encounter with Calderon, after Paul Adams's death, after the terror and threats in the valley, she knew there was only one way to deal with this bloody, explosive situation.

"If we don't do it, the cattlemen in the valley will," Hawthorne said.

He was right in that too, Jessie knew. "How many men does Beaumont have?" she asked.

"Less than ten," Hawthorne said. "He keeps most of them at the house, leaving Korman free to roam around town. Well, I suppose he has one less man, with Calderon gone."

"You're not going up against those men alone, Dennis. I suggest we talk to some of those other cattlemen in the Little Missouri Valley. They have a stake in this, too."

"This sounds like a lynch mob," Roosevelt blurted. As monstrous as this business had become, he could not allow his friends to spearhead a lynching.

"I don't want to see the Frenchman dead until he's answered some questions," Jessie said. "And I'm not advocating that we ride on his house with the local ranchers. I'm saying that when word about the Kings gets around, they're going to be hot for blood—the Marquis's blood. Somebody has to keep them together and prevent them from acting lawlessly. There will be bloodshed, Teddy, but no lynching. The Marquis de Beaumont and Niles Korman have chosen their own way. I want to make sure that when they go against the cattlemen, we're organized and united; that way it will be less easy for any one single ranch to be picked off."

"I say we kill the bastard tonight and have done with it," Hawthorne rasped.

"I know you're angry, Dennis," Jessie said.

"By God, I'm more than angry," he grated. "I've seen this happening for months, but now—the way they bush-whacked the Kings—I'm fed up. It's got to stop."

The four agreed to meet again, early in the morning. Roosevelt argued for caution. He wanted to wire the territorial marshal. Jessie and the others agreed, but knew it would be too late to do any good. It would take a lawman several days to get to Augusta, and by that time—

Ki went back to his room. Jessie lingered with Hawthorne. She was worried that his volatile temper would lead him to do something he shouldn't. At his door she said, "I want to talk with you, Dennis. May I?"

He opened the door and followed her inside.

"You think I'll do something stupid, is that it?" he challenged her.

"I'll take a drink, too," she said as he poured one for himself from the bottle he had taken from Roosevelt.

He smiled and poured her one, then handed her the glass as he said, "So, you want me to cool down, take it easy, not do anything I'll regret, is that it? Well, don't worry, Jessie." He raised his glass. "Here's to being careful and sensible and getting the bastard in the end."

"I just don't want to see you go get yourself killed for no good reason." She stroked his rugged face with her hands as he bent to kiss her. Their lips met and clung. He stood erect and took another swallow of whiskey. "That's the

Dennis Hawthorne I like best," she said seductively.

As they gazed at each other, the horror and violence they had encountered melted in the hot intensity of their need for each other. It was as if the threat that now hung directly over them made every passing moment even more tenuous, more valuable. For a while, at least, they could have each other. They had shared much in a very short time, and tomorrow they would share again in death's inevitable challenge. But tonight they were together, and no one could take that away from them.

Hawthorne smiled and said, "There isn't any Jessie Starbuck I don't like."

"There's a spoiled little girl you've never met." In the light from the lone oil lamp, her burnished hair shone golden and her eyes sparkled like emeralds. She felt his gaze, and color flooded her cheeks. Spoiled, yes, but she retained a sense of modesty that was ingrained in any properly raised girl.

"And there's a bitchy businesswoman who fights tooth and nail against anyone who challenges her right to run the business her father left her," she added.

"I still haven't heard anything I don't like. As for the spoiled girl, a good spanking will cure her. The businesswoman is out of my control—in fact, I'm not sure I want to meet her. I'm no good around money," he said.

"You're good in what counts, Dennis. I think even the Marquis is afraid of you because you don't bow down to him like nearly everyone else around here."

"Clark King didn't bow down to him, either," Hawthorne reminded her.

A sadness passed over Jessie again. "You should have seen that little baby, Dennis. An innocent child left with nothing, thanks to that killer Korman—and Beaumont. They're going to pay for it, I swear. I don't know how—"

"Seems to me you were on to an idea, gathering all the

ranchers in the valley to act together. But I'm not sure anybody could control them, once they get the killing fever."

"Do they have a leader among them?" Jessie wondered.

"A fellow named Evan Campbell, owns the Double Eight. He's been in the valley a long time. The Frenchie has tried several times to buy him out, but hasn't dared face Campbell himself. All the other ranchers look up to old Evan; he's tough as nails, a crusty son of a bitch who takes no shit from any man."

"I like the sound of him," Jessie mused. She said, "We'll talk to Campbell tomorrow. If anyone can keep the cattlemen in line, he sounds like the man. Think he'll be willing to join up with us?"

"If you're out to cut the Marquis down to size, he'll be tickled to ride with you," Hawthorne said.

She nodded, thinking to herself that it would take decisive leadership to defeat the Marquis and his hired guns. But with Hawthorne, Ki, and this Evan Campbell, there was a strong core of men who could lead the others in a tough situation. There were many grievances that had built up over the past year or so, and it looked as if they were coming to a head. So, if she could funnel them into a single confrontation, perhaps she could even get the Marquis to back off a bit and reduce his ambition . . . but she doubted it.

"Stop thinking, Jessie," Hawthorne said, interrupting her ruminations. He put his whiskey glass down and went to the bed. "Come here."

Jessie obeyed. She admired this man's strength and good looks, as well as his trail sense. Dennis Hawthorne was her idea of a real man—a specimen all too rare in her recent experience. Since her father's death, she had measured men against him and most had fallen far short. But Hawthorne was different, and she was irresistibly drawn to him.

Beside him on the bed, Jessie whispered, "Take me away from all this, Dennis." She raised her lips to his and they kissed again.

Hawthorne pressed her down onto the bed, gently easing himself on top of her. Their lips clung together as if forged in a farrier's fire. He felt her breasts rising against his own strong chest, the nipples hard and erect even through the fabric of her shirt. He held her to him, wanting to possess her, all of her, forever.

"Dennis," she pleaded, tearing her lips from his. "You're crushing me. I can hardly breathe." She laughed. "You're a bull."

"Thanks—I think." He lifted himself on his elbows. "Bulls have their good qualities, you know."

"Oh, I know," Jessie said. "How would the poor cows feel if there weren't any bulls?"

"Probably like I feel right now—ready to bust with wanting you, Jessie."

The two of them undressed and came together under the blanket on Hawthorne's bed. Jessie ran her hands over the flesh of his chest and back, beneath which his hard muscles bulged. She loved the feel of him, every contour and rippling muscle—and she loved the way he touched her in return, cupping her warm, round breasts and kissing them. She sighed, her eyes focused on his rugged face. Hawthorne needed a shave, and she raked her own peach-soft cheek across his stubble, kissing him on his chin.

Their naked bodies pressed hotly together. Jessie dropped her hand beneath the blanket and took hold of Hawthorne's hot, rigid manhood. He winced—half in pain and half in delight—as she squeezed it. Then she began gently pumping, sliding her fingers expertly along its engorged length, flicking over the head as a few droplets of fluid appeared there.

Hawthorne bent and kissed her neck, burying his face in the deep, soft curve, then working his way down, over her chest, nibbling on each breast in turn until she was moaning with pleasure. Jessie had to release his shaft as he slid down, bathing her belly with his lips and tongue. He lingered there only momentarily, pushing himself down, kissing her legs, the inside of her thighs, tasting the soft, fragrant fur on her mound of Venus.

Then Jessie gasped as she felt his tongue on her nether lips, probing gently but insistently. His beard scratched her pale inner thighs as he moved his head. The tongue penetrated her, pushing past the soft, slick petals of her exposed flower. She writhed wildly as he pressed harder, flicking his tongue up to touch the sensitive button that was the trigger of her passion.

"Oh, Dennis!" she cried. Her hands gripped his head and her legs fell apart. She could barely stand it, the electric sensation of his swirling, darting tongue at the core of her sex.

"Jesus—please—Dennis! Oh, stop it, please..." But she did not want him to stop. Suddenly she exploded from within, going liquid and limp as he continued to tongue her. Jessie tossed her head back on the pillow. Her body was racked with spasms and she tried to cry out, but could not. She came again and again.

Finally she found her voice. "Dennis, please—no more."

Hawthorne lifted himself beside her. She brought her face to hers, kissing him violently, tasting her own essence on his lips. "That felt so nice, Dennis, so nice!"

The man smiled and kissed her again. He, in turn, felt her soft hand take his sex and massage it, and the blood running hot within him made the shaft hard at her touch. She pulled at it and he lifted his hips to match her strokes. Jessie continued to squeeze and stroke it as she edged even closer to him. She put her mouth at Hawthorne's ear. "I want you inside me, Dennis. I want you to give me everything."

"Glad you asked, gal," he said with a pained half-smile. "I've never been readier."

He lifted himself over her, letting her guide him with an

136

eager hand. She spread her legs and lifted her pelvis to take him in. Then, with a quick, savage thrust, Hawthorne entered her. Jessie was wet and ready, and his length slid easily into her slick sheath.

She gripped his wide shoulders, her fingernails grazing his skin. She gazed up into his dark brown eyes and smiled, lifting her buttocks from the bed to take more of him in. "Yes, yes, do it to me like that," she urged.

His steel-hard manhood moved in and out of her tight chamber, driving them both to sweat and struggle like two lonely animals in the night, their need deepening with each thrust, everything but their passion forgotten for the moment. Hawthorne slowed his movements as Jessie reached down to hold his muscular buttocks and help control the pace. He grunted and pulled back, almost out of her, then pushed hard back in again, repeating this several times.

Hungrily, Jessie responded, lifting her pelvis and moving it slowly in a sensuous, circular motion. At the same time she drew up her legs and pressed them against his sides. She did not want this to end; she wanted him to make love to her forever—just like this.

"Love me, Dennis!" she exclaimed.

Together they established an urgent rhythm, bucking against each other unthinkingly, giving and taking all they had. Jessie's cries grew breathless and her eyes closed tightly.

Hawthorne's heart pounded in his chest, every last ounce of him behind each thrust, as he impaled the woman on his bed. He saw her writhing beneath him, her breasts heaving, her lips forming strange words that he could not hear. Never had he felt such intensity with a woman; never had he given so much to a woman, or received so much of her in return. This Jessie Starbuck was a phenomenon. And Hawthorne, who had never before professed love for any of his women, was on the verge of falling in love with her. *What is happening to me?* he wondered inwardly as he rode her.

Jessie's entire body stiffened and she saw the first flash of her orgasm as a bright light in her eyes. His big body loomed above her and she reached for his neck, pulling him down to kiss him. Then, as he thrust with all his strength into her, the flood broke over her frame, drowning her in white-hot liquid pleasure. Below, she contracted, squeezing him with her own love muscles.

Hawthorne felt her coming and could hold back no longer himself. He moved between her long legs, pressing his sword home again and again until he felt himself burst.

"Yes, come, Dennis . . . I want to feel you coming inside me!"

He obliged, thrusting with all his remaining strength. Her legs were wrapped around him, holding him in a love-vise from which he had no desire to escape. He was all hers, every drop of him. But soon there was no more to give and his movement slowed. Jessie pulled him down on top of her and lay there, crushing her breasts between their bodies, kissing her. The taste of her was better than the best whiskey. It made him hard again, and she felt his stiffening manhood against her leg.

"Don't you ever quit, Mr. Trail Guide?" she asked with a wink.

"Not until I've found what I'm after," he replied.

"I'm glad you were after me," she said. She clung to him, absorbing his strength and inhaling his masculine essence.

They lay like that for a long time. Hawthorne got up at one point and put out the lamp, then crawled back under the blanket with Jessie. He cradled her in his arms and after a while said, "Jessie, if it comes to shooting with Beaumont—I don't want you around. I don't want you to get hurt."

"Nonsense, Dennis," she said without hesitation. "Of course I'll do my share of the fighting." She lifted herself on one elbow. "Now, just because you made love to me, it doesn't give you the right to start telling me what to do," she added.

Hawthorne laughed. "Don't get hot at me, lady."

"I'm sorry, Dennis, but—but it's very important for me to see this through to the end, whatever that may be. I know how to handle a gun—better than some men I know. You saw me on the buffalo hunt; I didn't do anything foolish. I'm better than Teddy with a gun, and he's not bad."

"Not bad for an Eastern dude," amended Hawthorne. "But I'm not downgrading him—or you. It's just that I couldn't bear to see you hurt or anything. That's all I'm saying, Jessie."

"I know." She cupped his rough chin in her hand and kissed him on the forehead. "And I don't want you injured, either, my love." She lay back on the pillow and looked up at the darkened ceiling. "What's going to happen, Dennis?"

"I think the Marquis will fight back with everything he has, once he finds out that the independent ranchers are unified against him. He won't waste a second before sending his men out. That's what I think will happen."

"If only we could reason with him, get him to compromise. But Teddy failed at that last night. And if Teddy can't do it . . ."

"Beaumont wants it all, Jessie. He doesn't think in terms of anything less. He's no different than most rich men who think money rules the world."

"I guess I hoped he was. But the brutality of the King murders convinced me." A tear fell unwatched from her eye. "There was no reason on earth to kill those good people, Dennis."

"Except maybe to convince Jessie Starbuck to back off and leave the Badlands." Hawthorne stroked her soft, clean hair. "That's the only reason I can think of."

"Damn you, Dennis—always thinking the worst of people." She wanted to change the subject, to forget for as long as they could the impending conflict.

"I figure to live longer that way, ma'am."

"Well," said Jessie. "I'll just stay here and see that you survive at least tonight."

# Chapter 9

Word spread throughout the valley about the massacre at the Slash S. The fed-up ranchers agreed to attend a meeting the following night at Evan Campbell's Double Eight ranch, just three miles west of town. Jessie, Ki, and Hawthorne were there, along with a dozen others, at nine o'clock. Roosevelt stayed in Augusta to catch up on his voluminous correspondence.

"Never seen a man write so many goddamned letters," Hawthorne had said.

Now, though, the Easterner was the furthest thing from their minds as they sat among the angry group of Little Missouri Valley cattlemen. Several introduced themselves to Jessie and offered their condolences at the Kings' murders. They had all known and liked the soft-spoken ranch foreman and his wife and brother, and they were sick at the senseless end of the family. They knew it could have happened to any of them, rather than the Kings.

Campbell had a fine, big home and the ranchers met in the spacious living room, in front of a solid stone fireplace. The Double Eight was a thousand-acre spread on which the owner ran more than three thousand head of beef. He had established the ranch nearly fifteen years ago, and it was going strong, employing ten men full time and more at spring and fall roundups. Well respected among his peers, Campbell himself was an impressive man, tall and raw-boned, with a head full of wild gray hair; his blue-green Scots eyes blazed unequivocally when he was aroused, as he was now at this meeting. He stood in front of the gathering and, when everyone was present, started the proceedings.

"There ain't no formal cattlemen's organization here in the valley, and I ain't been elected to nothing myself, so if somebody else wants to get up here and run this meeting, he's got just as much right as me." He paused and gazed around the room. The other ranchers—a collection of men from their early thirties to their sixties, representing most of the independent spreads in the valley—made no move to oppose him, tacitly acknowledging his leadership.

Campbell, pulling himself up to his full height and pacing to and from in front of the fireplace, went on, "The purpose of this here meeting is to bring an end to some of the goings-on here in the valley that has folks on edge and not sure who's next. I'm referring to the King killings, in case any of you don't realize it, and to Jim Davidson's killing just a while back under, uh, mysterious circumstances." He spat the words out ironically. "You and me know there ain't no mystery to it, but that's another story. We didn't do nothing about it, and we should have." He eyed each man in the room, and Jessie, before continuing, "this time we're going to do something about it."

There was a scattering of applause in the room. And a few of the men nodded, their mouths set grimly in agreement. They gave Campbell their full attention.

"Now, everybody here knows everybody except maybe for the young lady from the Slash S, who is new here. Many of you met her pa years back when he came through and bought up the parcel north of here. She's Miss Jessie Starbuck. Welcome to the valley, ma'am."

Jessie stood and waved down the flutter of applause. She said, "Thank you, Mr. Campbell. I'm sorry I didn't meet you earlier—before this sad occasion. I'm glad we're having this meeting, because I have a few thoughts on the matters under discussion here. Let me just say that I'm willing to fight for the interests of all you ranchers. But let's not forget the legal processes that are available to fight lawlessness. I know you have no intention of letting this group become a lynch mob, Mr. Campbell, and I just want to say I think you're right. There's something badly wrong here in the valley, and if we all stand together we can lick the man who's causing the trouble—legally."

Then she turned to Ki. "I want to introduce all of you to my partner, Ki, who was a trusted friend of my father's and remains my friend, too. And I guess all of you already know Dennis Hawthorne," she added.

Murmurs of assent rippled through the room. A few of the men eyed Ki nervously, unsure just what to make of him, but no one moved to oppose the samurai's presence. If he was good enough for the young Miss Starbuck, they figured he was all right. Jessie sat back down, between Ki and Hawthorne. Evan Campbell continued the meeting.

"Thanks, Miss Starbuck, we all appreciate your being here—and Mr. Ki. Hawthorne there we all know. We've been keeping him away from our daughters for over a year now." The ranchers all laughed, and it helped ease the tension some. Jessie had never seen Hawthorne look sheepish until now, and she couldn't help smiling herself.

"As to our business—as Miss Starbuck says, whatever we choose to do, it's going to be legal. There ain't no local law to speak of, and the territorial law is spread pretty thin in these parts, so we got to act careful. I suggest, first of all, that we wire the capital to tell them we want something done—a deputy and a judge dispatched to Augusta. That way they can't say we've done anything illegal. All in favor of calling in the territorial law say aye."

There was a chorus of ayes.

"All not in favor say nay."

Silence.

"All right, then, I'll wire personal tomorrow morning." Campbell's gaze swept over the room. He was comfortable in a leadership position, despite his initial disclaimers; and it was apparent that the other ranchers looked up to him and considered him the natural spokesman.

"Next we got to decide what to do about our immediate problems. Some good people have been killed here—Davidson, the Kings, and the young fellow Adams that operated the newspaper. We all know why they was killed, too—because they didn't knuckle under to the Marquis up there on the bluff. I'm sorry to say I think Miss Starbuck's coming to the valley quickened some of this. She looks to me like a right smart lady who can't be fooled when it comes to the cattle business. She looks to me like a fighter. What do you say, ma'am?" Campbell gave her the floor.

Jessie rose and looked around the room, meeting the men's eyes. "Gentlemen, I've met the Marquis. I had dinner with him the other night. A more courtly and fine-living man you'll never run across. But there's something wrong with his mind—he wants to own every inch of ground in the Badlands. More than that, he'll stop at nothing to get what he wants. Only *we* can stop him—if we work together. Most of you were here long before Beaumont came, and I hope we'll all be here after he's gone.

"I suggest that a committee of three ride to the Marquis's house the day after tomorrow, after Mr. Campbell has telegraphed the capital, and present our grievances to the Frenchman, face to face. We won't threaten him, but we'll let him know exactly what we're up to. No surprises. And when he knows the law is coming, it'll be up to him to act. We can only pray he doesn't try to do something stupid."

"Hell, I still say we should hang the son of a bitch," one of the cattlemen grumbled aloud.

"There's going to be none of that kind of talk, Vance!" Campbell stormed. "We agreed this ain't no lynch mob. If you don't like it, you can get out." But the man didn't leave. "Anybody else?" His gaze swung across their faces. "We voted, goddamn it, and that's how we're going to do it. How many times do I have to tell you men?" He snorted in disgust. "I think the lady has a good idea—about the committee. Now, which of you wants to be on that committee? I'll take volunteers."

"You should be on it, Campbell," said the man called Vance. "You're the leader of us, ain't you?"

"Yeah!" cried a few others. And someone added, "Miss Starbuck should be on the committee, too. She's talked to the bastard herself." The same call of general assent was raised.

Campbell said, "What do you think, ma'am? You willing?"

"Sure," said Jessie, casting a sidelong glance at Ki. The quiet Oriental sat stoically; his eyes warned her to be careful. "I think the Marquis will listen to me. I just hope I don't tell him what I really think about what happened to Clark King and his family."

"Who else wants to come with us?" Campbell asked the men. "We still need one more cattleman—one with some guts. Who'll it be?"

The men looked back and forth among themselves, pointing fingers and suggesting this neighbor or that. They may have liked the idea of a face-to-face chat with Beaumont, but none of them really relished the idea of being there. Finally one man said, "I volunteer Vance over there. He talks good, and he drives a hard bargain. Once he tried to sell me a broken-down old cow pony for thirty dollars— and I almost paid!"

145

That brought a roar of laughter and some clapping. The rancher named Vance sat redfaced among the others, his head bent. One man slapped him on the back in support. Vance looked around and shrugged.

"What do you say, man?" Campbell asked him. "You in or out?"

"I guess if they all want me, I'm in," he mumbled. And so he became the third member of the committee.

"That settles it," declared Campbell. "Plato Vance, Miss Starbuck, and I will meet with the damned—I mean, with the Marquis—day after tomorrow. We have plenty of grievances and such to bring to him, and I want every man to have his say. Maybe we ought to write this down. Let's put together a list of specific things—night rustling, bribing the local boys not to work for us, making it hard for us to get bank loans—besides the killing. That'll be on the top of our list—telling him to call off his gun-dogs—but I want to have a whole string of things that will keep him stewing until the deputy and the judge get here. Come on now, boys, speak up. Darrow, there—what do you want on the list?"

Darrow, an emaciated tobacco chew of a man in his late fifties, rose slowly and looked around the room. He wasn't a public speaker, either, but he said, "Dadblamed Frenchman offered me ten thousand dollars for my place. I said I wouldn't sell, no way. Few days later one of my cows was cut open with a unborn calf still in her. Tell him to stop that, Campbell. A man can be pushed just so far." Darrow sat down.

"Attaboy, Darrow!" one man shouted. "You tell 'em."

"Somebody writing this down?" Campbell asked.

Hawthorne leaned over to Jessie and said, "We should've brought Teddy along. He'd do all the writing they asked him to."

One man volunteered to be secretary, and Campbell dug up some paper and a lead pencil. Campbell then asked each man individually what his particular grievance or circumstance was, and the secretary scribbled it all down, pausing only to whittle the point of the pencil sharp with his knife.

Jessie listened attentively to their stories. These men had worked like slaves to build their homes and ranches and raise their families, and now this strange-talking rich man had come in and built himself a town and a castle, and was threatening their very livelihood. Throwing money around freely, Beaumont had bought off a few men; but most, like those gathered in this room, had held out and suffered subtle but substantial damage.

It was clear that they feared the worst was yet to come — unless they put a stop to the terror themselves. One by one, they spilled their guts and found at least some solace in the unified front they were building. Acting alone — or, more likely, grumbling alone — they had never been able to achieve the confidence they were gaining now.

Campbell said, "Has every man had his say? Good. I don't think I need to tell you gentlemen that everything that has gone on here tonight is just amongst us — nobody else's business but ours. I'd recommend that you don't even tell your wives. Not that they'd be likely to pass word to the Frenchman, but let's not take any chances. Agreed?"

The men nodded. They saw the sense in what Campbell said, and agreed to keep quiet.

"Also, you'd all best make sure that your guns are clean and that there's plenty of ammunition in your houses — just in case. We got the best of intentions and we're all trying to do the right thing, calling in the law and all, but you never know when that fellow Niles Korman might come knocking at your door with some of his men — and they won't be coming to talk, believe me.

"We're all taking a big risk, just meeting together tonight. I'm proud to have you at my place, and I wouldn't want it nowhere else. Just remember — good intentions don't stop bullets. If you get fired on, fire back. We don't aim to start trouble—it's been started for us. We aim to protect our rightful property and our kin. Don't nobody try to be a hero. Call on your neighbor if you need help. Call on me whenever you need to. We're together now, and that's what counts most. They can't take that away from us. This meeting is over. Good night, boys."

Jessie stayed on, with Ki and Hawthorne, as the other men made their way out of the meeting, stopping to say a word or two to Campbell. When they were all gone, Evan Campbell came over to Jessie.

"You folks care for a drink?"

Jessie and Ki declined, but Hawthorne joined Campbell in a drink of whiskey.

The broad-shouldered rancher, more relaxed now, thanked Jessie again for coming. "It's real important to have the Slash S in with us on this. Your daddy made quite an impression when he came here and bought that land. Folks here respect the Starbuck name."

"I have a suspicion, Mr. Campbell," Jessie said, "that the same men who killed my father are behind the Marquis's dealings in the Little Missouri Valley. He's got big money to back him, and it might be coming from those so-called businessmen in Europe who are at war with the Starbuck interests throughout the West."

She went on to explain to the surprised rancher about the hated cartel—how these unscrupulous men, most of them from Prussia and the financial capitals of Western Europe, had seen a chance to capitalize on the great import-export trade that Alex Starbuck had established in the Far East, and how they continued now, after Starbuck's murder, to gain a strong foothold in the American West by destroying Starbuck companies wherever they could.

"It occurred to me the other day that the Marquis de Beaumont's father-in-law, this Heufer fellow, might be one of the principals in the cartel's operations in the United States. As a prominent New York banker, he is in a perfect position to funnel money into their various enterprises. I checked my book to see if I had any record of him, but . . ."

Jessie told Hawthorne and Campbell how Alex Starbuck had kept a running record of cartel-connected individuals in the United States and abroad, updating his information continuously as he ran afoul of cartel operations. She told them of the copy she had made of her father's diary after his death, which contained the same information in abbreviated form, and in which she carried on the task of compiling data on the octopuslike criminal syndicate's members and activities. Unfortunately, the black-leather-bound notebook in her saddlebag contained no listing of the Marquis de Beaumont, his wife, or his father-in-law. Of course, if any of them proved to be in league with the cartel, this information would be added to that which she already possessed; it was her hope that someday this list of names and foul deeds could be used to end forever the cartel's ultimate and most vicious scheme—the overthrow of the government of the United States of America.

Campbell scratched his chin. "Sounds pretty farfetched, Miss Starbuck. Not that I disbelieve what you're saying, but—out here in the Badlands, in this valley?"

"The valley, as you know, is a prime cattle-raising area— and it's just the type of investment this cartel is interested in making the most of. Where do you think the Marquis gets the financial support to make his bids for these ranches?"

Hawthorne, who remained skeptical, said, "But you don't have proof of any of it, Jessie. Much as it might be true—"

"It is true," she blazed.

Ki, who had sat silent throughout the meeting, watching the men, listening to the proceedings, surprised them all by speaking up now. "Jessie and I have learned from our experience with these evil men how they operate. Even if the

149

cartel is not behind the Frenchman, big-money interests are."

"Now that's true enough," Campbell acknowledged. "And we know at least that he's dangerous as hell—especially with all those gunnies on his payroll."

"Dennis," Jessie added quietly, "I'm not making any of this up. Lord knows, we have plenty to worry about already."

"Sure, Jessie. But, Christ Almighty—Germans running around trying to grab control of the valley, and to destroy you—it's just a bit hard to swallow, is all I'm saying."

"We'll find out plenty the day after tomorrow," Campbell said. He got up to refill his drink, and poured Hawthorne another healthy shot too.

Jessie said, "What do you know about this man Vance who is to go with us?"

"Plato Vance? He's not a bad fellow," said the old rancher. "Not the best man in the valley, but he seems honest, and I know he's a hard worker. He has six young'uns over at his spread, the Rocking V, south of here."

"He didn't seem all that eager to join up with our committee," Jessie commented. "I just want to make sure we can count on him."

Campbell pondered that, then said, "As far as any of us can trust each other, I'll vouch for Vance. He's got as much to lose as any of us."

"I suppose so," Jessie said. But inside her there was a suspicion stirring. *Why the hell can't I let go of my own worries and learn to trust without questioning everybody?* she asked herself. Maybe she had been betrayed too often, or had been fighting the damned cartel for too long. Still, there was something about Plato Vance that didn't seem right to her.

"Ki and me will ride with you if you want us to," Hawthorne suggested.

Campbell said, "Maybe it'd be a good thing if you came

to the house, but stayed outside. Wouldn't hurt to have our backsides covered—just in case Beaumont tries anything funny."

Roosevelt was in a quandary. What in blazes should he do? He read the telegraph message again—for the tenth time. The message worried him sick, but could he leave Augusta now, just when this business with the Marquis de Beaumont was coming to a head? If there was violence, if any of his friends were hurt, how could he run home when they might need him?

He waited until Jessie and the two men returned from their meeting at the Double Eight. They were a somber enough crew, and he was reluctant to tell them his newest troubles.

Jessie told him all about the meeting. She said the "committee" would ride to the house the day after tomorrow, and no one knew what would happen after that.

"Well, that should be a bully occasion. Show the man your strength and tell him you're not going to take any more of his hooliganism."

Jessie sighed, "I don't think it's going to be that easy, Teddy. I just have a bad feeling about the whole thing. The ranchers seemed like good men, but unprepared, really, if anything goes terribly wrong."

"You mean if violence breaks out?" Roosevelt queried.

"That's exactly what she means," said Hawthorne. "You got anything to drink around here, Mr. Roosevelt?"

"I'm afraid I don't," the New Yorker said. He turned to Jessie. "And I'm afraid I have some bad news of my own. It's—it's my wife, Alice—I received this wire tonight. It looks as if I must return home immediately." He handed the telegraph message to Jessie, who read it with concern.

"You've got to go back to New York," she said without equivocation.

"But if I do that—I feel as if I'm abandoning you at a

very bad time. I can't leave you here to fight this battle, if it comes to a battle."

As he spoke, the Easterner's eyes gleamed behind the spectacles, and his mouth moved rapidly beneath the trimmed mustache. He resembled nothing more than a boy who was afraid of being left behind while his father went off on a hunting trip. There was more, though—a genuine concern for Jessie, Hawthorne, and Ki.

"Your wife, Teddy," Jessie reminded him.

Roosevelt looked at her somewhat sheepishly, and nodded. "I know. My first duty is to her—and the baby." Then, for the first time, the import of the message finally hit him with full force. "The baby . . ."

Hawthorne said, "I'm going to get a bottle. I think we could use a drink."

Jessie comforted the stricken New Yorker, sitting with him on the edge of his bed. "They wouldn't have wired you if it wasn't serious," she said, "but who knows? By the time you get there, everything could be fine. Think of it that way."

"Damnation!" Roosevelt cursed, his fists balled. "If anything happens to Alice and I'm not there—I'll never forgive myself. Perhaps I never should have come here. She didn't want me to come."

"Don't go punishing yourself, Teddy," Jessie said. "You couldn't have known anything would happen."

The worry and anxiety sank deeper, though, and when Dennis Hawthorne came back with a bottle of whiskey, she took a drink herself and made sure Roosevelt drank a healthy measure of the liquor. It seemed to calm him some. Hawthorne poured himself a large glassful and downed it in three swallows. He was already calm enough—but his mood had darkened at the news of Roosevelt's situation. He smelled something wrong, but couldn't put his finger on it. He took another drink.

"Now don't you get drunk on me, Dennis," Jessie chided him gently. Here she was with two grown men who were acting like grounded ranch hands. She didn't like whatever it was that was poisoning the air here in Augusta. Luckily, Ki retained his senses and refused any whiskey. She stayed long enough to see that Roosevelt prepared to get to bed so he'd be fresh for his journey tomorrow. Then she left him alone.

Hawthorne and Ki followed her from the room.

Korman stalked his man alone. He wanted this one for himself. He hated spies and squealers—though he'd done his share of both in his time. To him, men like this were the lowest form of life, well worth eliminating. He checked the action on his Winchester .44-40 repeating rifle; it worked perfectly, and quietly. He wondered, as he followed the man on horseback, staying well back in the darkness, whether to backshoot the bastard or to confront him face to face and listen to him whine before putting a bullet in his brain. He had a while yet to decide. Plato Vance was still more than a mile from his ranch. . . .

Vance had come to the Marquis's home directly after the rancher's meeting, under cover of darkness. Nervous, hat in hand, his gray-black hair plastered down on his head, the cowman had waited in the foyer to be shown into the Frenchman's library. Korman had been there in the library with Beaumont when Vance was admitted.

"Well, sir, this is an unexpected pleasure, as you Americans say." The Marquis was at his oily, genteel best, rising to clasp his visitor's hand. "To what do I owe your visit at such an unusual hour?" He gestured for Vance to sit on one of the plush, comfortable chairs near the desk.

Vance did so, holding his sweat-stained hat over his knees. "Well, Mr.—er, Marquis, I just thought you might appreciate something I have to tell you. I thought—that is,

I decided it might be best—telling you, that is—and maybe even save some folks from trouble that don't want it, see?"

"That sounds quite noble, Mr. Vance. But I am hard put to decipher just what it is you seem so bent on telling me. It might help if you spelled it out in plain English." The Marquis took his place behind the imposing desk, his fingers neatly drawn together beneath his smoothly shaven, aristocratic chin.

He arched an eyebrow at Niles Korman, who stood nearby, just at Vance's left shoulder. Korman looked sleek in his black suit, with the coattails swept back to reveal his deadly twin companions, the Colt revolvers he wore cross-draw style. The weapons were level with Vance's eyes.

Vance started to talk, a sort of gurgling noise rising in his throat. A tide of perspiration formed on his lined brow. Beaumont interrupted him before he could begin. "Would you care for a drink, Mr. Vance?" He lifted a silver bell from his desk and a black servant appeared at the faint tinkle. The Negro filled three glasses with dark, dry wine. Vance swallowed some, and that helped to clear his throat.

"Thanks, Mr. Marquis," the rancher said. "I was near choked up there for a minute."

"I could see that, sir. Now, if you would kindly tell me—"

"Yes, sir. You see, I just come from a meeting over at Evan Campbell's Double Eight, and there was a lot of cattlemen over there, men from the valley, about a dozen of them, I reckon." All of this came out in one breath, and Vance gulped some air and slurped some wine and went on. "And Campbell, he ran the meeting and told the men that we—they—better do something, but he said he didn't want nothing done legal—I mean illegal. That's what he said."

"*What* did he say?" Korman sneered softly, over Vance's shoulder.

154

Vance looked up quickly at the sharp-faced enforcer and struggled to get the words right. "Well, Campbell said that we wasn't going to stand no more from—that is, from you, Mr. Marquis, buying all of us out and taking hold of the whole valley for yourself and leaving us with nothing."

"My dear Mr. Vance," the Marquis intoned, his voice a low, assuring balm for the man's nerves. "I should never be able to live with myself if I deprived hard-working men such as yourself of everything you have struggled for. Why should I do such a thing?"

"I dunno." Vance shrugged. "But that's what Campbell said. And the other men agreed, it seemed like. Leastways, they all voted to so something about it."

"*All* of them voted?" Beaumont asked. "How did you vote, Mr. Vance?"

"Hell, I voted with the rest of them. I didn't want to look like a—"

"Horse's ass," Korman provided.

The rancher ignored him. "There wasn't nothing else I could do," he said.

"And in this esteemed senate of ranch owners, what was it you decided—so democratically—to do about me?" Although his inflection was the politest and courtliest possible, the Marquis's words were dipped in venom.

"We—they decided to put together a committee to come and talk to you."

"That was awful nice of them, to think of that. Maybe we can have tea, boss. And we can sit here and talk like ladies. You like that idea, Mr. Vance?" Korman said.

"Who is on this committee?" Beaumont asked, ignoring the gunman's barbs.

Vance swallowed hard before answering. "Well, Campbell's on it. And the Starbuck gal, the one with hair the color of my pa's polished copper watch."

"Jessica Starbuck?" the Marquis rose from his chair, his

fists clenched. "She was at your meeting? She is on this committee?"

"Yes," the rancher replied. Now he was regretting that he had come here. What did he expect to gain from coming to Beaumont? Money? More land? Safety and security? It occurred to him in a flash that he would get none of these things. But he had come this far and couldn't turn back now. He said, "The other one was me. They volunteered me for their committee."

"But you decided to make yourself a one-man committee, is that it?" asked Korman.

"Yeah—I mean, no. I just thought it best . . ."

Vance was at a loss for words, all talked out. He could feel Korman's cold, steely glare on his neck, and it scared him. Looking into the Marquis's ice-blue eyes didn't help, either.

"Honest, Mr. Marquis, sir, I don't want trouble. I got a family and we got a nice ranch and we work hard. I was thinking, though, about maybe reconsidering that offer you made me a while back—for the ranch, I mean. Maybe it'd be best if I sort of took it. Hell, I can work a ranch anywheres."

"Perhaps you are unaware, Mr. Vance, that my offer was good only for twenty-four hours from the time it was tendered." The Marquis spoke slowly and precisely, so that each word had its full impact upon Vance. "I'm afraid"—as the palms went up—"that the offer no longer stands."

So Vance had left the chateau empty-handed—and frightened. He mounted his horse and wished there were some moonlight, but there was none. He rode away at a quick clip, not realizing that Korman was close behind on his backtrail. . . .

Now Korman made his move. He kneed his mount gently and began to close the gap, careful to keep the horse's pace moderate in order to advance as silently as possible. When he was within fifty yards he thought Vance had heard him as the lead rider slowed and looked back. The darkness shrouded Korman adequately, though, and he reined in his horse and patted its neck to keep it quiet. Vance moved on. Korman stealthily closed in.

They were less than a half-mile from Vance's place now. Korman thought he could see a light in the distance, across the flat stretch of grassland where the ranch house should be. He had been out here once before, many months ago, to make that offer from the Marquis to which Vance had referred. He had half expected the rancher to take the money then, noting the scared-rabbit look in Vance's watery eyes. But Plato Vance, in front of his wife and children, had acted brave and righteous and refused the money, declaring that he was bound to stay at the Rocking V, which he had built with his own hands and intended to leave to his sons. Nothing could move him, he had said then. Nothing.

A grin slashed across Korman's face at the recollection. He was within twenty yards now. It was time. He urged his horse forward, and the animal kicked up dust along the narrow pathway over which they rode. This time Vance heard Korman clearly. Vance's horse snorted, sensing trouble, and its rider reined in and turned, waiting. He made no move for his weapon, a saddle-sheathed rifle.

Korman's gun, cradled in his arm, swung toward the rancher. He slowed his horse, and then stopped it when he came abreast of Vance. Korman looked at the rancher, who was little more than a dark outline now against the blue-black sky. There was no wind tonight, no sound at all except the breathing of the two horses.

"I figured you were going to come after me, Korman." There was no fear in Vance's voice, only a dead certainty. He sat his horse stoically, unmoving, waiting.

"That was mighty smart of you, Vance. I always said you were a smart one. Just not quite smart enough for your own good, is all. You would've been smarter to leave a long time ago, when you still could."

"I know that now. Doesn't do me much good to know that, but I do."

"No, not much good."

Korman felt like smoking a cigar, but he didn't have one. He had that queer taste in his mouth that he sometimes had, when he was about to do some damage. Funny how it still happened to him after all these years and after all the men he had killed. It tasted dry and rough, like oats.

"What do you want with me, Korman? I told your boss I would go if he wanted. Even without the money. I got my family to think about."

"You should have thought about them before. It's a mite late now. If you was as smart as I once made you out to be, you would've thought of them before."

Vance dropped his eyes to the earth. It seemed a long way down from where he sat his horse. His head hung like a pinecone ready to drop off the tree. He didn't say anything. There wasn't anything he could say now.

Korman dismounted, keeping the barrel of his Winchester canted up, aimed at the defeated rancher. "I want you down off your horse, Vance." The rancher hesitated. Korman said, "Now."

Plato Vance dropped the reins. He swung down, slowly and deliberately. The gunman's rifle followed his movements. It seemed to him an eternity before both feet touched the ground. The night was thick with darkness and he wished he could see better—he wanted to see Korman's face. He still found it hard to believe that the man could kill him out here in cold blood, though he knew better.

The wire-thin gunman grunted something and stepped carefully around to Vance's left side. He said, "Take your rifle out of the boot. Do it cautious and slow and keep your hand clear of the trigger. Try anything funny—"

The rancher obeyed, unsheathing the long-barreled gun, holding it gingerly by the stock, pushing it out in front of himself. Korman snatched it from him. Vance's empty hand hung there for a moment and then he drew it in and stood stiff and still. Korman whacked the rancher's horse on the rump with the rifle, and the animal whickered and took off for the house, following the same trail it had taken so many times before. Korman and Vance were alone now, except for the gunman's mount.

Korman hefted Vance's rifle in his left hand. He chambered a bullet and squeezed the trigger, shooting into the air. The gunshot shattered the density of the black night. Then he threw the rifle at Vance's feet.

"Should've been smarter, Vance. Save a lot of people a lot of grief."

"I only wanted to do what was right," Vance said, his throat constricted painfully, choking the words out.

"Sometimes that's all right. But not this time."

With deliberate precision, Korman aimed his .44-40, raising the well-balanced rifle to his shoulder, sighting on Vance's face, between the eyes. He squeezed off a careful shot that penetrated the rancher's brain.

Vance crumpled to the earth, dead. Korman quickly mounted his horse and pulled away, leaving the body there for somebody else to find.

# Chapter 10

"The Marquis knows everything," Ki said.

"The only question now is who will make the first move," Jessie replied.

It was the following night. Roosevelt was gone, having vowed to return one day, as soon as he could. Plato Vance's death had been reported in Augusta. A cloud of tension had settled over the town. Jessie felt the stares as she and Hawthorne walked in the streets. Ki had visited Olivia, who still refused to leave town, instead threatening to seek her own vengeance against Korman. Ki, Jessie, and Hawthorne were talking at one of the tables in the Dog's Eye. Inside the saloon, the atmosphere was gloomy.

O'Hare said, "You can count on me, Miss Jessie. I'm sick of this manure that damned Marquis fellow and Korman and the others are shoveling. Hell, I'm ready to fight back."

"Thanks," she said. "But let's wait till Campbell gets here before we load our guns."

Dennis Hawthorne took a pull at his whiskey and took a deep drag on his hand-rolled cigarette. He was itching for a fight now, knowing it was inevitable. He watched the door impatiently for Campbell. When he glanced over at Jessie, she smiled at him. He reminded himself that he couldn't drink too much tonight—just in case. *Damn*, he cursed to himself, weary of this protracted showdown, *when will it end?*

For his part, Ki understood the others' frustration. He, too, felt that the decisive confrontation was at hand. Unable to convince Olivia that now was indeed the time to leave Augusta, he worried about her; she remained determined to exact revenge from Niles Korman for his longtime abuse of her. The samurai sat at the table and sharpened his *tanto* blade on a small whetstone, preparing himself spiritually and mentally, ready to discuss strategy once Campbell arrived.

The old rawboned rancher arrived late. The battered batwing doors swung closed behind him with a rusty squeal. He strode to the table—practically the only one in the tavern that was occupied—with a brisk, businesslike step. But they all could see that the lines in his face had been gouged deeper and his eyes seemed a bit more sunken in his ruddy face. He wore a Remington revolver at his hip and carried a double-barreled Greener shotgun in his big hand.

"Care if I join you in destroying that bottle?" he asked, pointing to the half-empty whiskey bottle on the table. He pulled up a chair.

"Help yourself," said O'Hare. "On the house tonight."

"Thanks, O'Hare. What are you folks discussing?" Campbell crooked his elbow and tossed the shot down with a well-practiced move.

"We were waiting for you," Jessie said, "before making any definite plans. Have you heard any more news?"

"Nothing tonight," said Campbell. "What do you hear?"

Ki repeated for Campbell what he had learned from Olivia. Korman had tried, late last night, to see her, shouting at her window from the street. She had not answered him, but he knew she was there. He had told her the Marquis was committed to all-out war now, and that her friends were going to pay for their open opposition to the rich Frenchman.

Korman had said, "And tell the members of the committee they're short one member!"

"I'm not surprised," Campbell growled. "That murdering son of a bitch. He must have made Vance talk, then shot him. Damn his skinny hide! I'll be pleased to put a bullet in him myself."

"Not if I get to him first," said Hawthorne.

Jessie smiled wanly. "There are plenty who want a crack at him. But I'm just as worried about his other men. I haven't seen any of them around. How many are there?"

O'Hare said, "I count a total of six, now that the Mexican is gone. They keep mostly to themselves, drinking in here sometimes, but staying at the house the rest of the time."

"I'd say that's right," Evan Campbell affirmed. "My boys have kept an eye on their comings and goings. A rough crew, all right. Look like they've been recruited from hell, some of them."

Knowing that the Marquis himself was reputedly an excellent shot, Jessie calculated that there would be at least eight men to worry about if it came to exchanging lead. She wondered aloud, "What are the chances they'll make the first move—ride against one of the ranchers or come into town looking for trouble?"

"Very little," Hawthorne said. "I think they'll hole up at the big house and wait for us to make the first move. The Marquis probably still thinks we'll back down, now that the committee lost Vance. He's got nothing to lose by sitting tight, at least for now."

Campbell drew his elbows from the table and tilted back in his chair. He said, "We'll just have to appoint a new committee member. I'm set on riding to the house tomorrow like we planned. If the bastard wants us to come to him, I say we do it, and face him down."

"I'll be on your committee," O'Hare blurted. "Hell, you need someone from the town. It's not just you cowmen that

Beaumont is bearing down on. We feel it here, too."

Jessie looked at Campbell. "I don't object if you don't. But I think we should inform the ranchers what we're doing."

"To tell you the truth, Miss Starbuck, those other men are scared to death since Vance was shot. I tried to talk to some of them today, and they've all clammed up, having second thoughts about the big plans from the meeting last night. They're nearly ready to cave in to Beaumont."

"All of them?" Hawthorne asked.

"Pretty near," Campbell acknowledged.

"Goddamn," O'Hare breathed. "What is it that gets into people when the stakes get high?"

Jessie, though, tried to look at it realistically. These men had more than their own lives at stake. Like Vance, they had families, men on their payrolls. It had to be a tough decision for them; they weren't being dishonorable, she figured, just prudent. "That leaves it up to us," she said, resigned.

"Listen here, Miss Starbuck," Campbell put in. "Maybe we better rethink this committee business—I mean your being on it and all. I'd sure as hell hate to see you get hurt over this. You're new here in the valley, and—"

"I'm not afraid, Mr. Campbell. And even if I have never been here before, my father was here and he invested in the Slash S. The Kings worked for me. I've got a lot on the line myself here."

"What I mean is, you being a woman and all—maybe it's not such a good idea."

Jessie's eyes were sparks of green fire, and her nostrils flared. "It makes no damned difference that I'm a woman!" Her fist came down on the table. Other patrons in the Dog's Eye looked up from their drinks and cards.

The men around her were stunned into silence for a moment. Then O'Hare said, "It won't make no difference to that bastard Beaumont, that's for sure."

Ki said, "Jessie, none of the choices we make here are easy ones. Mr. Campbell is concerned for you, that's all."

The old rancher nodded vigorously. "That's a fact, Miss Jessie."

"All right. Sorry I took it the wrong way," Jessie said, backing away a little. She liked Campbell and realized he was old enough to be her own father, and he probably saw her as just a girl. When the time came, she'd have to prove to him what she was made of.

The five of them decided to meet at dawn here at O'Hare's saloon and prepare what they would say to the Marquis later in the morning. All of them, though, doubted there would be much talking by that time. And they were resigned to the fact that they'd better be well armed and carrying plenty of ammunition. It wasn't going to be a tea party. . . .

Campbell went home and Jessie, Ki, and Hawthorne left O'Hare to close his place up. At the hotel, Ki went immediately to his room to take some much-needed sleep. Jessie lingered at her door with Hawthorne. She saw that he was restless, keyed up, perhaps too intent on the looming confrontation.

"Dennis, why don't you come inside and lie down— with me."

His deep brown eyes betrayed the need he also felt. But something held him back. "I'll be damned if I know what's come over me, Jessie," he said. "I've probably been drinking too much—got to quit that." His eyes fell to the floor. "I—I like you a lot, Jessie—a hell of a lot, I guess. What Campbell said tonight, about your being a woman and all— I thought he was right. In a way."

He looked up, his eyes meeting hers. She was so damned beautiful! If she got hurt, he'd by-God see that somebody paid for it. The idea of it frightened him, he had to admit. He didn't want to see one lovely hair on her harmed. Never had he felt this way before, about any woman he had ever met. Whatever it was, it was like a fire in his gut.

"What are you saying, Dennis?" she asked him frankly. She saw the hurt in his face. It made him more vulnerable, more human, and she liked him for it. After all, he was a man—handsome and strong, yes, but subject to fears and deep feelings as well. "Tell me what's on your mind," she prodded him.

"Hell, if I knew, I'd tell you, gal." He raked a large hand through the tangle of tobacco-brown curls on his head. "It's just that I'd go crazy if anything happened to you. You mean something special to me. And believe me, to say it costs me something. You're not like any girl I've ever known. I've never loved another girl, neither."

"Oh, Dennis," she breathed. She put her arms around him and he held her tightly to him. "Come in with me. I need you."

At her touch, with her fine, shapely body pressed to his, Hawthorne relented. "I suppose I'd be a damned fool not to stay with you, Jessie. I need you something powerful."

Taking the tall, rugged man by the hand, she led him into her dark room and closed and latched the door behind them. And as she lay locked in his strong arms on the bed, she thanked God that she had this man and prayed that Hawthorne and Ki and the rest of them lived past noon tomorrow.


As they mounted up outside O'Hare's place after having a bite to eat and some hot coffee, Olivia emerged and said she was going with them. She was dressed in a pair of pants—probably her brother's—tied to her waist with rope, and a floppy hat into which she had stuffed her hair.

Evan Campbell looked at her as though she were crazy; O'Hare muttered an oath and told her to get back inside, she wasn't going anywhere.

Ki said, "Olivia, why are you doing this?" Hooking his

Japanese bow over the pommel, he dismounted and went to her.

Jessie looked at Dennis Hawthorne, who shrugged as if to say, *I don't know what the hell this is about.* They sat their saddles as Ki talked to the girl.

Olivia's face was bruised and her mouth was set. Ki could say nothing to stop her and he knew why she had to go: to see that Korman was punished if the meeting turned to fighting, which she had no doubt it would.

"You don't have a horse," said Ki.

But Olivia said she would get one at the livery. She had already talked to the boy there and he had one saddled and ready for her.

Ki turned to Jessie. "She will follow us if we do not let her ride with us."

Hawthorne took an extra rifle from the right-hand boot and gave it to the girl. "Stay out of the way if there's any shooting," he warned her. "And don't use this unless you're shooting at something in particular. Understand?"

Olivia nodded. Ki lifted her up behind him on his horse, where she rode with them to the livery stable to pick up her mount. It was ready, as she had told them it would be.

Campbell pushed his hat back on his head and wiped his brow, grumbling, "All these confounded women . . ."

The trail to the top of the bluff was a tortuous one, and the riders had to watch both forward and behind for ambush. They weren't scared—here in the bright light of the new day—but they realized it paid to be extra careful. The Marquis knew they were coming. Hawthorne took the lead, followed by Jessie and Ki. Olivia came next, and after her rode O'Hare and Campbell. Overhead the sky was bright and clear, with a lovely patch of cottony cloud floating far above them.

They rode in silence, their weapons holstered but close at hand. All of them carried rifles except Ki, who was armed

167

only with his bow and *ebira* quiver of war arrows.

As the party topped the bluff, Hawthorne reined in and allowed everyone to catch up and gather around him. Their horses blew mightily after the rough climb. Jessie, Campbell, and O'Hare took the lead for the final approach to the house. Ahead stood the chateau, a queer sight in its isolation and bizarre construction.

Jessie's mind was racing. They were going to go through with their original plan to talk first, and she hoped it wouldn't come to open fighting. But she knew there was little chance of a peaceable resolution. It sickened her to think that there had to be more bloodshed, and she desperately searched her mind for a way around it. Everything depended on Beaumont—how he would react to their challenge would set the stage for what was to follow. And she couldn't imagine that he would react with anything but force of arms. Well, at least the party was prepared, if not eager, for that.

She looked at the strange house as it loomed closer. It represented the dreams of a madman, she realized now. She was certain now that it had been built with the backing of the men who had killed her father; if nothing else, the very look of the place seemed to bear the mark of the cartel. Even in the clean sunlight, the place looked evil, like one of those haunted castles in Old Europe, teeming with ghosts and restless, malevolent spirits. She wasn't superstitious, but a deathly chill took hold of her as she gazed at the chateau. She wondered how she had ever set foot in there and eaten Beaumont's food and drunk his wine. It all seemed so unreal and faraway now as she approached it again.

Campbell and O'Hare flanked her. The rancher turned to Ki, Hawthorne, and the girl. He said, "Stay here, about fifty yards from the house. Don't take out your weapons unless we order you to." He pointed to a stand of stunted trees to the party's right, just about the only shelter around. It was closer to the house, about twenty yards. He said,

168

"We'll regroup over there if shooting starts. Be ready to move quick."

The old cattleman looked at Olivia. "Gal, you don't belong here. If you want to leave—"

"No," she said firmly, touching her rifle.

"All right." Campbell wheeled his mount around beside Jessie, and he and Jessie and Hawthorne rode slowly toward the house.

"Be awful damned careful," Hawthorne said under his breath.

As the three riders approached, there was no sign of life in the big chateau. But Jessie and the others felt that they were being watched closely, their every move taken in by unseen eyes. She called out, "Hullo the house!"

At first there was no response. Then, unexpectedly, the front door opened and Beaumont himself stepped out. He was dressed bizarrely in a fancy "frontiersman's" costume of beaded and fringed buckskin, with a big white hat and polished boots. Under his arm he carried a rifle canted downward. And directly behind him stood Niles Korman, a black specter watching them over his boss's shoulder.

"Good morning, gentlemen, Miss Starbuck." The Marquis gave a courtly sort of bow. "I must order you to remove yourselves from my property—immediately. You were not invited here and, I'm sorry to say, you are not welcome."

"We've come to talk, Marquis," Jessie stated.

"We don't want trouble," Evan Campbell added, reining in his frisky mount.

"Neither do I, sir," said Beaumont. "Therefore I advise you to leave."

"We represent the cattlemen of the valley," Jessie persisted. "We were elected by them to—"

"Ah!" Beaumont's eyes lit up with humor and he gave out a short laugh. "Your precious democratic process at work, I presume. Well, I happen to know that these cattle-

169

men you claim to represent do not approve of your actions. My men have spoken to them, and—"

"You mean your boys have put the fear of the devil in them," Campbell growled.

"My men have *spoken* to them, I said." The Marquis was giving no ground. "However you wish to put it, I happen to know that the families in the valley have repudiated you and your so-called committee. You do not represent them. You do not represent anyone."

"You know why we're here," said Jessie, the anger rising within her. She shifted in the saddle. "We're not leaving until we get some satisfaction."

"I'll give you all the satisfaction you crave," Korman taunted from inside the doorway.

"Keep your filthy mouth shut, mister," O'Hare spat back, his face red.

"Have you come to trade insults with Mr. Korman?" the Marquis asked casually. "Surely you could do that in your own place of business, Mr. O'Hare."

"That's not why we came, goddamn it," Campbell rasped. "We aim to parley with you, Beaumont. We want you to quit harassing our people and sending your boys out to hurt them or threaten them. And this killing must stop. We were here before you showed up, and we'll be here long after you're in your grave."

"Do you intend to put me in my grave, sir?" the Frenchman sneered. He was getting hot himself, as evidenced by the occasional twitching of his mustache.

The committee was getting no place, Jessie could see. The Marquis was being stubborn and Campbell and O'Hare were being sorely tested to control their tempers. The clear September air hung heavy between them and the house. Out of the corner of her eye she spied movement at one of the second-story windows. That was where Beaumont's men were, she figured; probably there was one stationed at each window. She didn't like this setup one bit.

Jessie apprised Campbell of the situation, whispering urgently. He glanced up at the windows and nodded slightly.

"I told you this was no place for a woman," he muttered.

The Marquis shouted, "I'm advising all of you to ride away—now. You are trespassing. Anything you wish to say may be written in a letter for my private consideration. Otherwise, you have no business here." And with that he turned and strode back into the house, the fringe on his fancy jacket fluttering in his wake.

Korman remained standing where he was, eyeing the defiant group. "You heard what he said, people. Get the hell out of here."

Frustrated, angry, stalemated, they looked at one another. Jessie wanted to go in there and drag the pompous Frenchman out and make him talk. And after that she would take care of the gunman in the black suit. She saw the same thoughts reflected in her partners' eyes. But that was not why they had come here—and the Marquis had simply refused to hear them out. What was left for them to do?

"Let's go," Campbell said finally. "Looks like we'll have to wait for the territorial law to deal with these people. Much as I hate to say it." He shot a baleful glance at Korman in the door, then reined his horse around.

Jessie and O'Hare followed him, turning to join the others, who waited farther back. A feeling of impotence washed over them—along with the feeling that several guns were aimed at their backs.

As they started to move, Korman called, "You can leave that Mex slut here for me and the boys, but the rest of you ride on back to town!"

That was too much for O'Hare. The saloonkeeper wheeled his mount around, blazing with anger. "Shut your lying mouth, Korman—or I'll shut it for you, permanent."

"Aw, come on, Irishman, you oughta know better. She's

171

a fine piece of ass—as if you haven't tried her yourself. Why don't you share, like a nice fella?"

Riled to his limit, O'Hare spurred his horse forward, unsheathing his rifle. A big man, he moved awkwardly, unaccustomed to fast action. He managed to get his long gun up and to work a round into the chamber as he charged, puffing loudly. But Korman, stationary and prepared, was quicker.

The black-clad gunman stepped forward and raised his Winchester. He sighted on the big man coming toward him.

Jessie shouted for O'Hare to watch out, but to no avail. The burly tavern owner dug his heels into the animal's flanks and forged ahead toward the house, his own gun at the ready, his eyes seeing nothing but the loathsome son of a bitch who had insulted Olivia.

Korman let him get nearly up to the doorway before he blasted O'Hare from the saddle with a single shot. The big man took the bullet in his chest and reeled back, falling off his shying horse and hitting the ground with an awful thud.

The others watched in openmouthed horror, frozen in disbelief as the scene unfolded. Hawthorne shouted for Jessie to get back. Campbell raised his own rifle and got a shot off, barely missing Korman and taking a chunk out of the front door. Korman ducked inside and avoided a second bullet that the rancher fired hastily.

Jessie pulled her horse around and headed back to where the others were, near the sheltering trees. She turned to see that Campbell was getting away, too. The old rancher whipped his horse into action and was right behind her. As she looked back at the house, Jessie saw six windows being thrown open. Six gun barrels then appeared in the open windows and began blasting away at the retreating pair. She ducked and heard the bullets whistle past. The horse lunged toward the trees. By a miracle, it seemed, she made it safely. Campbell, too, survived the barrage and joined the others behind the only cover they could find.

They all dismounted. Hawthorne shooed the horses away, out of range. The animals galloped off in a lather, whickering in fear. They wouldn't go too far, the guide knew—but he didn't want to endanger them in this senseless fight.

The party spread out behind the trees as lead rained down on them. Korman's men blasted away furiously, and it was a full minute before fire could be returned by the embattled group in the copse.

Olivia, especially, was frightened, falling to the ground with her hands over her ears. Ki dove from his horse and went to her, urging her to stay down, taking his own position in front of her to offer more protection. He brought his long bow smoothly into place and nocked an arrow, aiming for the gunman in the window closest to him. He released the shaft and it shot off in a low arc.

It missed, but the samurai already had another arrow ready. He adjusted his aim and loosed the second arrow. This time he found his mark; the shaft flew straight and sure into its target's neck. Ki could see the man's hand reach up spasmodically to clutch the protruding shaft, his mouth open, blood spurting from the severed artery. Then the man fell out of sight.

Meanwhile, Hawthorne sided Jessie, dust and powder smoke streaking their faces. This was all-out war, and Hawthorne felt somewhat relieved that it had finally come—that there was no more talk, no more planning, just fighting. Crouched low behind the gnarled trunk of a short pine tree, he took aim with his .50-caliber Sharps. The big rifle boomed as he sent lead into the house. The gun was more than powerful enough for this range—and when he hit a man with the big slug from the buffalo gun, there would be no question about the result.

He sighted on Korman in the doorway, but missed with his first two shots. Then he felt the return fire from the other hardcases buzzing past his head like angry bees.

Hawthorne switched his aim from Korman to a fat-faced

man in a first-floor window. The man was pumping bullets like mad, spraying the party behind the trees. Hawthorne took his time and held in his breath as he squeezed the trigger. He felt the powerful gun kick against his shoulder and could almost see the big-caliber slug hit home, taking off a piece of the man's skull. The man pitched forward and hung over the windowsill, his rifle dropping to the ground outside.

Jessie turned to see where Campbell had landed. The grizzled rancher, fighting for breath in the heat of the action, was off to her left, without much cover. But the man didn't seem to care much where he was, as long as he could reply to these bastards with lead. He was working his old Henry repeating rifle with grave efficiency, splintering the window frames and sending the men inside ducking for cover. The look on his face was a mixture of rage and glee. Probably it had been a long time since he had been in a real gunfight like this—and a part of him was enjoying it immensely.

The hot wind of flying lead brought Jessie's attention back to defending her own position. She chambered a round and fired her rifle, chipping some wood into the face of one of the hardcases in the window. She could see their faces, those men, like white coins swinging in the boxlike windows—straightforward, even easy targets, but for the heavy fire they kept dishing out.

She jacked another cartridge into the chamber and fired again. This time she saw that she had winged the man. He dropped his weapon and clutched his left arm with a grimace. But before she could get off another shot, he had moved away and was no longer visible. He would resurface at another window, she figured.

Ki killed another man with a swift-flying arrow. Now three of the Marquis's men were down, but there was no sign of the Frenchman himself. He was well inside the house, either directing the action or hiding under a table; the outsiders couldn't tell which.

Korman, though, was very visible, boldly emerging from his cover inside the door to blaze a few shots and then slide back again. No one could get a piece of him, though they all tried.

Suddenly, Jessie heard a shout close by. She turned to see Dennis Hawthorne slump to the ground, groaning. She scooted over to him. "Dennis! Are you hit?" Hot tears stung her eyes.

"God—damn—" he gritted, his face bathed in sweat. He clutched his right leg. Blood oozed out between his fingers. He had taken a slug in his thigh.

Jessie tore her bandanna from around her neck and quickly wrapped the wound, bullets knifing through the air around her. Hawthorne went pale as shock set in. She made him lie back, well behind the tree. Angrily she hunkered down beside him and began firing into the house. There were only four of them left inside, not including the Marquis. She blinked the tears away as she tried to take aim.

Several yards away, Ki was working his bow, spending arrows with caution. After the first two men he had downed, he was having bad luck. The gunmen were staying just out of range of the arrows. He had only a dozen left. He changed his target, nocking a shaft and aiming for Korman's position, waiting for the hatchet-faced man to show himself in the door. He heard Olivia behind him, sobbing. She had not expected anything like this, and the rifle lay at her side, useless. He knew she shouldn't have come, but nothing and nobody could have stopped her.

Then he saw Korman step out, saw the smoke from his rifle as he pumped three quick shots that dug up the earth near Ki. Without hesitation, the Oriental let the arrow fly, and as he released it he knew his aim was true. As Korman lowered his gun, the shaft found its home—in the skinny gunman's chest.

Korman's jaw dropped open and his hands went clutching for the arrow. He tried to yank it out but could not. He toppled facedown in the doorway, unbelieving in his own death.

Ki let out a high-pitched shout of victory that brought a momentary silence to the field of battle. Now there were only two men in the chateau windows.

Campbell, who had been denied a trophy thus far, renewed his efforts. The veteran rancher brought his Henry around and focused on a red-haired man in a corner window on the second floor of the house. He could almost feel the man's eyes on him as he pumped round after round at the enemy. Finally his furious, singleminded effort paid off. Two bullets smashed into his antagonist, one entering his eye, leaving a dark, blood-gushing hole, the other punching into his chest. In a spray of blood and gore, the red-haired man disappeared for good.

The tide of battle had turned now, and the party didn't let up, pursuing their advantage, Jessie and Campbell driving the remaining gunman from his position.

A sudden, heavy silence descended as they finally ceased firing. Campbell rose slowly, steadying himself with a hand resting on a tree trunk as he squinted through the drifting gunsmoke, looking for signs of life. There was nothing.

Then at last there came a sound—the hooves of a lone horse from somewhere on the other side of the house. Campbell and Ki scrambled out from cover. The rancher kept his rifle trained on the house as Ki advanced in front of him. Jessie stayed back with Hawthorne and Olivia. Ki raced around the side of the chateau in time to see the Marquis de Beaumont, still decked out in his fancy Wild West costume, riding hell-for-leather into the Badlands.

# Chapter 11

There hadn't been much time to think, but Jessie knew what she wanted to do. She made sure Hawthorne would be all right, then dispatched Olivia to try to round up the horses. The girl obeyed unquestioningly and was able to round the animals up in several minutes—riding her own horse back and leading the others. Jessie asked Evan Campbell to help Hawthorne back to town, to a doctor.

"And where the hell're you going, Miss Jessie?" he asked, grim-faced.

"Ki and I are riding after Beaumont," she said.

"Now what the hell—"

Wearily she said, "Don't give me any trouble, Mr. Campbell. Get these people back to Augusta. Poor Mr. O'Hare, too. He'll be needing a proper burial. Ki and I have to ride."

In unspoken agreement, Ki had brought their horses around. Jessie checked to see that she had enough ammunition, then mounted up. She pulled the animal around and dug her heels into its flanks and galloped off, Ki riding away in her wake.

They couldn't let the Frenchman gain too much of a lead. It was just past noon, and she wanted to catch him before nightfall. She and Ki pressed their horses to move faster. They kept their eyes on the trail, which was clearly marked and easy to follow. The Marquis was no frontiersman, despite his pretentions, and he couldn't have lost a three-year-old riding a mule, with the sign he left behind.

He was riding fast, though, and for an hour Ki and Jessie kept their own horses at nearly full speed. Across the pitted land they traveled wordlessly, each knowing what was in the other's mind: simply to catch up with Beaumont and bring him back to town alive, if possible, to stand trial. They stopped once to water the horses, but pressed on. To delay was to chance losing their man among the gullies, buttes, and hidden caves of the Badlands. Whether or not the Frenchman had a sharp trail sense, he had a keen sense of self-preservation. They had to be careful, too, that the Marquis didn't lead them into an ambush, doubling back on his trail and lying in wait for them.

Jessie mulled over the entire tragic situation as she rode, her eyes never wavering from the wild landscape before her. O'Hare was dead. She was sorry as hell about that; he had been a good man, even a friend in the short time she and Ki had known him, and now he was gone. Just the last of Korman's victims. Hawthorne was hurt—how badly she did not yet know. And inside the chateau were four dead men and one injured man, as well as Korman. She felt her stomach turn. It was a waste. She hoped Campbell could get Hawthorne and Olivia back safely—and O'Hare's remains.

How many people dead, how many lives ruined, how much human misery inflicted? All because of one man's insatiable greed. Vance, Adams, the rancher Davidson, the poor King family. She pressed on beside Ki as he read the sign like an experienced scout.

"His horse has a loose shoe," Ki said, breaking the tense silence of the open trail. He pointed to the marks that showed

Beaumont's horse favoring the left hind leg.

"He'll ride it till it's dead," muttered Jessie. "And then what?"

"He will be waiting for us," said Ki simply.

He halted his mount and surveyed the trail in front of them. They were heading north now, in the direction of the Slash S. The river was a mile or so to the east. The land was scored with colorful ridges and gouged with cutbacks, giving the pursued man plenty of places to hide. They would have to be careful, for Beaumont might be getting desperate now, as his horse slowed down. He'd attack without warning, so they must be prepared for anything.

A half hour later, as Jessie and Ki topped a sloping bank, a single shot rang out, echoing against the hills. Jessie's horse trumpeted in pain and crashed to the earth beneath her. She was just able to jump free as it fell, or else it would have pinned her to the ground with its body.

The shot came from a nearby ridge, crested with pines. Ki jumped from his saddle to help Jessie as the Marquis opened up, spraying lead all around them.

Jessie lay flat on the ground behind her horse. She was glad she had reloaded her rifle, for now she was able to answer Beaumont's fire. She sent three rounds over the ridge, keeping the Frenchman down as Ki dismounted and slapped his horse to get the animal away, out of the line of fire. He joined her behind the fallen animal.

Jessie kept up her fire as best she could while Ki prepared an arrow. He nocked the shaft in the bowstring and waited. Beaumont raised his head, hatless now, and peppered lead at their position, the bullets thudding into the big horse's carcass. Ki waited for Jessie to get two shots away; then she ducked low to reload her weapon.

The samurai gauged his target and shot the arrow in a very high, lofting arc so that it would descend on the other side of the ridge. He followed with a quick second arrow, in a slightly lower arc. Then he waited. Jessie held her fire.

A muffled noise came from the other side of the ridge, and there was no more gunfire. Either Ki's arrows had found their target, or the Frenchman was playing a game with them to lure them into the open. For ten full minutes they waited. Still there was no sound, no movement, no action at all from behind the ridge.

Ki said, "Stay here, Jessie."

Reluctantly she agreed. "Be careful, Ki. It might be a trick."

"I know," he said. He rose and darted across the open ground toward the ridge.

She watched, biting her lower lip, praying that nothing would happen to her friend. Then she saw him cautiously climb the ridge and disappear over the other side. For a few tense seconds she was ready to charge ahead after Ki— until she heard him shout that all was clear. Jessie bolted to the ridge.

She found Ki standing over Beaumont. The Frenchman had taken one of the samurai's arrows in his left shoulder, just below the collarbone. The shaft was buried deeply in his flesh and he winced in pain, his eyes closed, his face bloodless and shiny with perspiration. Blood trickled from the deep wound, staining his white buckskin jacket. When he opened his eyes there was hate there, and defeat. He looked ready to kill them both—if only he could. But his rifle lay just out of reach, where Ki had kicked it.

"You—got what you—wanted," Beaumont said through his teeth.

"I never wanted any of this," Jessie said wearily. "You brought it all on yourself."

The Marquis, his fancy outfit soiled from his frantic ride and his desperate last stand, tried to sit up. Ki helped him, but Beaumont was weak. He looked down at the arrow sticking out of him and said, "Get this thing—out of me."

Ki glanced at Jessie, then turned back to the Marquis and said, "We can't do that. If we did, you'd likely bleed to death before we could get you back to Augusta. A doctor will have to cut the arrow out of you and cauterize the wound. It will be painful, but you will not die, as much as you deserve it."

Ki then went off to find Beaumont's horse and his own, leaving Jessie to watch their prisoner.

"I want to know one thing, Beaumont," she said.

"What?" he groaned.

"Did you act alone in this, or did you have backers?"

His blue eyes were cold and nearly lifeless. He said, "I think you already know the answer to that."

"I want to hear it from you. Were they behind you?"

"Yes," he hissed violently. "Yes—" He glared at her without remorse. "I could have done it—could have had it all—if it were not for you."

"I don't think so," said Jessie. "The people in the valley would have stopped you sooner or later."

"Those spineless half-men. They did not understand me. I could have made something out of this godforsaken place. They are too stupid, too weak..." He groaned in agony, his face white as chalk.

Ki returned with the horses. They tied the Frenchman into his saddle and Jessie rode with Ki on his mount. Together they led their downed enemy on a slow, silent trip back to Augusta—back to justice. Halfway there, the Marquis collapsed from loss of blood and they had to bind him more firmly to his mount so that he wouldn't fall off.

When they could see the town in the distance, Jessie said to Ki, "I've been thinking—the Slash S needs a new foreman. Do you suppose Dennis would take the job if I offered it to him?"

"There's no way to tell, except by asking the man," Ki replied.

181

Jessie, even more bone-weary now than when she had first set eyes on Augusta several days ago, smiled to herself. *No,* she thought, *Dennis won't take the job. Not at first. But maybe I can talk him into it.* Her smile deepened and she told her partner, "I'm going to do my damnedest to persuade him."

Watch for

LONE STAR AND THE SAN ANTONIO RAID

seventeenth novel in the exciting
LONE STAR
series from Jove

*coming in December!*

# LONGARM

**Explore the exciting Old West with one of the men who made it wild!**

| | | |
|---|---|---|
| ___06953-1 | LONGARM ON THE SANTA FE #36 | $2.25 |
| ___06954-X | LONGARM AND THE STALKING CORPSE #37 | $2.25 |
| ___06955-8 | LONGARM AND THE COMANCHEROS #38 | $2.25 |
| ___07412-8 | LONGARM AND THE DEVIL'S RAILROAD #39 | $2.50 |
| ___07413-6 | LONGARM IN SILVER CITY #40 | $2.50 |
| ___07070-X | LONGARM ON THE BARBARY COAST #41 | $2.25 |
| ___07538-8 | LONGARM AND THE MOONSHINERS #42 | $2.50 |
| ___07525-6 | LONGARM IN YUMA #43 | $2.50 |
| ___07431-4 | LONGARM IN BOULDER CANYON #44 | $2.50 |
| ___07543-4 | LONGARM IN DEADWOOD #45 | $2.50 |
| ___07425-X | LONGARM AND THE GREAT TRAIN ROBBERY #46 | $2.50 |
| ___07418-7 | LONGARM IN THE BADLANDS #47 | $2.50 |
| ___07414-4 | LONGARM IN THE BIG THICKET #48 | $2.50 |
| ___07522-1 | LONGARM AND THE EASTERN DUDES #49 | $2.50 |
| ___06251-0 | LONGARM IN THE BIG BEND #50 | $2.25 |
| ___07523-X | LONGARM AND THE SNAKE DANCERS #51 | $2.50 |
| ___06253-7 | LONGARM ON THE GREAT DIVIDE #52 | $2.25 |
| ___06254-5 | LONGARM AND THE BUCKSKIN ROGUE #53 | $2.25 |
| ___06255-3 | LONGARM AND THE CALICO KID #54 | $2.25 |
| ___07545-0 | LONGARM AND THE FRENCH ACTRESS #55 | $2.50 |
| ___07528-0 | LONGARM AND THE OUTLAW LAWMAN #56 | $2.50 |
| ___06258-8 | LONGARM AND THE BOUNTY HUNTERS #57 | $2.50 |
| ___06259-6 | LONGARM IN NO MAN'S LAND #58 | $2.50 |
| ___06260-X | LONGARM AND THE BIG OUTFIT #59 | $2.50 |
| ___06261-8 | LONGARM AND SANTA ANNA'S GOLD #60 | $2.50 |

*Available at your local bookstore or return this form to:*

**JOVE**
*Book Mailing Service*
*P.O. Box 690, Rockville Centre, NY 11571*

Please send me the titles checked above. I enclose _____ Include 75¢ for postage and handling if one book is ordered; 25¢ per book for two or more not to exceed $1.75. California, Illinois, New York and Tennessee residents please add sales tax.

NAME _____

ADDRESS _____

CITY _____ STATE/ZIP _____

(allow six weeks for delivery.)                                    6